The Girl Aviators' Sky Cruise

Margaret Burnham

The Girl Aviators' Sky Cruise

CHAPTER I

A NEW VENTURE IN SANDY BEACH

"It isn't to be a barn; that's one thing certain. Who ever saw a barn with skylights on it?"

Peggy Prescott, in a pretty, fluffy morning dress of pale green, which set off her blonde beauty to perfection, laid down her racket, and, leaving the tennis-court, joined her brother Roy at the picket fence. The lad, bronzed and toughened by his trip to the Nevada desert, was leaning upon the paling, gazing down the dusty road.

About a quarter of a mile away was the object of his contemplation — a big, new structure, painted a staring red. It had no windows, but in front were great sliding doors. On its flat roof the forms of a dozen or more glazed skylights upreared themselves jauntily.

"No, it's a work-shop of some sort. But what? Old man Harding is interested in it, that's one thing sure. I heard, too, that while we were away, cases of machinery had arrived and been delivered there, and that active work of some sort had been going forward ever since," rejoined Roy, who was clad in white tennis flannels, with white shoes and an outing shirt, set off by a dark-red necktie.

"See Roy," cried Peggy suddenly, "they're putting up some sort of sign on it, or else I'm very much mistaken."

"So they are. I see men on some ladders, and now, look Peg, they are carrying up a big board with something painted on it. Perhaps at last the mystery will be solved, as they say in the dime novels."

"Can you read the printing on that sign?" inquired Peggy.

"Not a word. I can see the letters to know that they are printed characters, but that's all. Tell you what, Peg, just run and get those glasses we used on the desert — there's a good fellow — and we'll soon find out."

"Isn't that just like a brother? Always sending his long-suffering sister on his errands."

"Why, you know you are dying with curiosity yourself, to know what's on that signboard," parried Roy.

"And I suppose you're not," pouted Peggy in mock indignation. "However, I'll get the field glasses to oblige you — just once."

"As if you won't try to secure the first peek through them!" laughed Roy, as sunny Peggy tripped off across the lawn to a big shed in the rear of the Prescott home, where the aeroplanes and their appurtenances were kept.

She soon was back with the field glasses, and, as Roy had prophesied, raised them to her eyes first. Having adjusted the focus, she scrutinized the sign carefully. By this time the big board had been raised horizontally above the doors and was being fixed in position.

Suddenly Peggy gave a little squeal of astonishment and lowered the magnifiers.

"Well, what is it?" chaffed Roy; "an anarchist bomb factory or an establishment for raising goats, or something that will "butt in" just as much on our peace and quiet, or — —"

"Roy Prescott," enunciated Peggy, severely shaking one pink-tipped finger under Roy's freckled nose, "this is not a subject for jesting."

"Never more serious in my life, Sis. If you could have seen your own face as you peeked through those glasses — —"

Peggy stuffed the binoculars into her brother's brown hands.

"Here, look for yourself," she ordered. Her voice was so imperious that Roy obeyed immediately.

An instant later his sister's expression of dumfounded amazement was mirrored on his own straightforward, good-looking countenance.

"Well, as Bud used to say out West, 'if that ain't the beatingest'!" he gasped.

3

"What did you read?" demanded Peggy breathlessly. "Repeat it so that I may be sure my eyes didn't play me a trick."

"Not likely, Sis; the letters are big enough. They show up on that red painted barn of a place like a big freckle on a pretty girl's chin."

Then he repeated slowly, mimicking a boy reciting a lesson:

"The Mortlake Aeroplane Company. Well, wouldn't that jar you?"

"Roy!" reproved Peggy.

"There's no other way to express it, Sis," protested the boy. "Why, that's the concern that's been advertising so much recently. Just to think, it was right at our door, and we never knew it."

"And that hateful old Mr. Harding is interested in it, too, oh!"

The exclamation and its intonation expressed Peggy's dislike of the gentleman mentioned.

"It's a scheme oh his part to make trouble for us, I'll bet on it," burst out Roy. "But this time I guess it's no phantom airship, but the real thing. What time is that naval lieutenant coming to look over the Prescott aeroplane, Peggy?"

"Some time to-day. He mentioned no particular hour."

"Do you think it possible that he is also going to take in that outfit down the road?"

"It wouldn't surprise me. Maybe that's why they are just putting up the sign. They evidently have refrained from doing so till now in order to keep the nature of their business secret. If we hadn't come back from Nevada sooner than we expected, we might not have known anything about it till the navy had investigated and—approved."

Far down the road, beyond the big red building, came a whirl of dust. From it presently emerged a big maroon car. Peggy scrutinized it through the glasses.

4

"Mr. Harding is in that auto," she said, rather quietly for Peggy, as the car came to a stop in front of the Mortlake Aeroplane Manufacturing Company's plant.

Shortly before Peggy and Roy Prescott, their aunt, Miss Sallie Prescott, with whom they made their home, and their chums, Jess and Jimsy Bancroft, had returned from the Nevada alkali wastes, the red building which engaged their attention that morning had caused a good deal of speculation in the humdrum Long Island village of Sandy Beach. In the first place, coincident with the completion of the building, a new element had been introduced into the little community by the arrival of several keen-eyed, close-mouthed men, who boarded at the local hotel and were understood to be employees at the new building. But what the nature of their employment was to be, even the keenest of the village "cross examiners" had failed to elicit.

Before long, within the freshly painted wooden walls, still sticky with pigment, there could be heard, all day, and sometimes far into the night, the buzz and whir of machinery and other more mystic sounds. The village was on tenter-hooks of curiosity, but there being no side windows to peer through, and a watchman of ferocious aspect stationed at the door, their inquisitiveness was, perforce, unsatisfied. Not even a sign appeared on the building to indicate the nature of the industry carried on within, and its employees continued to observe the stoniest of silences. They herded together, ignoring all attempts to draw them into conversation. What Peggy and Roy had observed that day had been the first outward sign of the inward business.

From the throbbing automobile, which the boy and girl had observed draw up in front of the Mortlake plant, a man of advanced age alighted, whose yellow skin was stretched tightly, like a drumhead, over his bony face. From the new building, at the same time, there emerged a short, stout personage, garbed in overalls. But the fine quality of his linen, and a diamond pin, which nestled in the silken folds of his capacious necktie, showed as clearly as did his self-assertive manner, that the newcomer was by no means an ordinary workman.

His face was pouchy and heavy, although the whole appearance of the man was by no means ill-looking. His cheeks and chin were clean shaven, the close-cut beard showing bluely under the coarse skin. For the rest, his hair was black and thick, slightly streaked with gray, and heavy eyebrows as dark in hue as his hair, overhung a pair of shrewd, gray eyes like small pent-houses. The man was Eugene Mortlake, the brains of the Mortlake Company. The individual who had just descended from the automobile, throwing a word to the chauffeur over his shoulder, was a person we have met before—Mr. Harding, the banker and local magnate of Sandy Beach, whose money it was that had financed the new aeroplane concern.

CHAPTER II

MR HARDING DECLARES HIMSELF

Readers of the first volume of this series, "The Girl Aviators and The Phantom Airship," will recall Mr. Harding. They will also be likely to recollect his son, Fanning, who made so much trouble for Peggy Prescott and her brother, culminating in a daring attempt to "bluff" them out of entering a competition for a big aerial prize by constructing a phantom aeroplane. Fanning's part in the mystery of the stolen jewels of Mrs. Bancroft, the mother of Jess and Jimsy, will likewise be probably held in memory by those who perused that volume. The elder Harding's part in the attempt to coerce the young Prescotts into parting with their aerial secrets, consisted in trying to foreclose a mortgage he held on the Prescott home, with the alternative of Roy turning over to him the blue prints and descriptions of his devices left the lad by his dead father. How the elder Harding was routed and how the Girl Aviator, Peggy Prescott, came into her own, was all told in this volume. Since that time Mr. Harding's revengeful nature had brooded over what he chose to fancy were his wrongs. What the fruit of his moody and mean meditations was to be, the Mortlake plant, which he had financed, was, in part, the answer.

In the volume referred to, it was also related how Peter Bell, an old hermit, had been discovered by means of the Prescott aeroplane, and restored to his brother, a wealthy mining magnate.

In the second volume of the Girl Aviators, we saw what came of the meeting between James Bell, the westerner, and the young flying folk. By the agency of the aeroplane, a mine—otherwise inaccessible—had been opened up by Mr. Bell in a remote part of the desert hills of Nevada. The aeroplane and Peggy Prescott played an important part in their adventures and perils. Notably so, when in a neck-to-neck dash with an express train, the aeroplane won out in a race to file the location papers of the mine at Monument Rocks. The rescue of a desert wanderer from a terrible death on the alkali, and the routing of a gang of rascally outlaws were also set forth in full in that book, which was called "The Girl Aviators on Golden Wings."

The present story commences soon after the return of the party from the Far West, when they were much surprised — as has been said — to observe the mushroom-like rise of the Mortlake factory. But of what the new plant was to mean to them, and how intimately they were to be brought in contact with it, none of them guessed.

"Well, Mortlake," observed Mr. Harding, in his harsh, squeaky voice — not unlike the complaint of a long unused door, "well, Mortlake, we are getting ahead, I see."

The two men had, by this time, passed within the big sliding doors of the freshly-painted shed, and now stood in a maze of machinery and strange looking bits of apparatus. From skylights in the roof — there were no side windows to gratify the inquisitive — the sunlight streamed down on three or four partially completed aircraft. With their yellow wings of vulcanized cloth, and their slender bodies, like long tails, they resembled so many dragon-flies, or "devil's darning needles," assembled in conclave upon the level floor. At the farther end of the shed was a small blast furnace, shooting upward a livid, blue spout of flame, which roared savagely. Actively engaged at their various tasks at lathes and work-benches, were a dozen or more overalled mechanics, the most skillful in their line that could be gathered. Here and there were the motors, the driving power of the "dragon flies." The engines glistened with new paint and bright brass and copper parts. Behind them were ranged big propellers of laminated, or joined wood, in stripes of brown and yellow timber. Altogether, the Mortlake plant was as complete a one for the manufacture of aerial machines as could have been found in the country.

"Yes, we are getting along, Mr. Harding," returned Mortlake, "and it's time, too. By the way, Lieut. Bradbury is due here at noon. I want to have everything as far advanced as possible in time for his visit. You won't mind accompanying me then, while I oversee the workmen?"

8

Followed by Mr. Harding, he made an active, nervous tour of the work-benches, dropping a reproof here and a nod of commendation or advice there.

When he saw a chance, Mr. Harding spoke.

"So the government really means to give us an opportunity to show the worth of our machines?" he grated out, rubbing his hands as if washing them in some sort of invisible soap.

"Yes, so it seems. At any rate, they notified me that this officer would be here to-day to inspect the place. It means a great deal for us if the government consents to adopt our form of machine for the naval experiments."

"To us! To you, you mean," echoed Mr. Harding, with an unpleasant laugh. "I've put enough capital into this thing now, Mortlake. I'm not the man to throw good money after bad. If we are defeated by any other make of machine at the tests I mean to sell the whole thing and at least realize what I've put into it."

Mortlake turned a little pale under his swarthy skin. He rubbed his blue chin nervously.

"Why, you wouldn't chuck us over now, Mr. Harding," he said deprecatingly. "It was at your solicitation that the plant was put up here, and I had relied on you for unlimited support. Why did you go into the manufacture of aerial machines, if you didn't mean to stick it out?"

"I had two reasons," was the rejoinder, in tones as cold as a frigid blast of wind, "one was that I thought it was certain we should capture the government contract, and the other was — well, I had a little grudge I wished to satisfy."

"But we will capture the government business. I am not afraid. There is no machine to touch the Mortlake that I know of — —"

"Yes, there is," interrupted Mr. Harding; "a machine that may be able to discount it in every way."

"Nonsense! Where is such an aeroplane?" "Within a quarter of a mile from here. To be accurate, young Prescott's—you know whom I mean?"

The other nodded abstractedly.

"Well, that youth has a monoplane that has already caused me a lot of trouble." The old man's yellow skin darkened with anger, and his blue pinpoints of eyes grew flinty. "It was partly out of revenge that I decided to start up an opposition business to his. He was in the West till a few days ago, and I never dreamed that he would return till I had secured the government contract. But I am now informed—oh, I have ears everywhere in Sandy Beach—that this boy and his sister, who is in a kind of partnership with him have had the audacity to offer their machine for the government tests also."

"Audacity," muttered Mortlake under his breath, but Harding's keen ears caught the remark.

"It is audacity," agreed the leathern-faced old financier; "and it's audacity that we must find some way to checkmate. I've never had a business rival yet that I haven't broken into submission or crushed, and a boy and a girl are not going to outwit me now. They did it once, I admit, but this time I shall arrange things differently."

"You mean——"

"That I intend to cinch that government business."

"But what if, as you fear, the Prescotts have a superior aeroplane?"

"My dear Mortlake," the pin-point eyes almost closed, and the thin, bloodless lips drew together in a tight line, "if they have a superior machine, we must arrange so that nobody but ourselves is ever aware of the fact."

With a throaty gurgle, that might, or might not, have been meant for a chuckle, the old man glided through the doors, which, by this time, he had reached, and sliding rather than stepping into his machine, gave the chauffeur some orders. Mortlake, a peculiar expression on his face, looked after the car as it chugged off and then turned and re-entered the shop. His head was bent, and he seemed to be lost in deep thought.

CHAPTER III

A NAVAL VISITOR

Roy had departed, on an errand, for town. Peggy, indolently enjoying the perfect drowsiness of noonday, was reclining in a gayly colored hammock suspended between two regal maple trees on the lawn. In her hand was a book. On a taboret by her side was a big pink box full of chocolates.

The girl was not reading, however. Her blue eyes were staring straight up through the delicate green tracery of the big maples, at the sky above. She watched, with lazy fascination, tiny white clouds drifting slowly across the blue, like tiny argosies of the heavens. Her mind was far away from Sandy Beach and its peaceful surroundings. The young girl's thoughts were of the desert, the bleak, arid wastes of alkali, which lay so far behind them now. Almost like events that had happened in another life.

Suddenly she was aroused from her reverie by a voice—a remarkably pleasant voice:

"I beg your pardon. Is this the Prescott house?"

"Good gracious, a man!" exclaimed Peggy to herself, getting out of the hammock as gracefully as she could, and with a rather flushed face.

At the gate stood a rickety station hack, which had approached on the soft, dusty road almost noiselessly. Just stepping out of it was a sunburned young man, very upright in carriage, and dressed in a light-gray suit, with a jaunty straw hat. He carried a bamboo cane, which he switched somewhat nervously as the pretty girl advanced toward him across the velvet-like lawn.

"I am Lieut. Bradbury of the navy," said the newcomer, and Peggy noted that his whole appearance was as pleasant and wholesome as his voice. "I came—er in response to your letter to the department, in regard to the forthcoming trials of aeroplanes for the service."

"Oh, yes," exclaimed Peggy, smothering an inclination to giggle, "we—I—that is——"

"I presume that I have called at the right place," said the young officer, with a smile. "They told me——"

"Oh, come in, won't you?" suddenly requested the embarrassed Peggy. "The sun is fearfully hot. Won't you have a straw hat—I mean a seat?"

"Thank you," replied Lieut. Bradbury, gravely sitting in a garden bench at the foot of one of the big maples. His eyes fell on the book Peggy had been reading. It was a treatise on aeronautics.

"It isn't possible that you are R. Prescott?" he asked, glancing up quickly.

"Oh, no. I am only a humble helper. R. Prescott is in town. He—he will be back shortly."

"Indeed. I had hoped to see him personally. I was anxious to inspect the Prescott type of monoplane before visiting another aeroplane plant in this neighborhood, the—the——" The officer drew out a small morocco covered notebook and referred to it.

"The Mortlake Aeroplane Company," he concluded.

"Oh, yes. They are just down the road, within a stone's throw of here. You can see the place from here; that big barn-like structure," volunteered Peggy, heartily wishing that the Mortlake plant had been a hundred miles away.

"Indeed. That's very convenient. I shall be able to make an early train back to New York. Do you suppose that Mr. Prescott will be long?"

"I don't really know. He shouldn't be unless he is delayed. But in the meantime I can show you the aeroplane, if you wish."

"Ah!" the officer glanced at this girl curiously, "but you know what I particularly desired was a practical demonstration."

"A flight?"

"Yes, if it were possible."

"I think it can be arranged."

"You have an aviator attached to your place, then?"

Peggy laughed musically. She had quite recovered from her embarrassment now.

"No. I guess it's an aviatress—if there is such a word. You see I——"

"You!"

"Oh, yes. I have flown quite a good deal recently. I think it is the most delightful sport there is."

A sudden light seemed to break over the young officer.

"Are you Miss Margaret Prescott, the girl aviator I have read so much about in the technical publications?"

"I believe I am," smiled Peggy; "but here comes my aunt, Miss Sallie Prescott."

As she spoke, Miss Prescott, in a soft gown of cool white material, emerged from the house. Peggy went through the ceremony of introduction, after which they all directed their steps to the large shed in which the Prescott machines were kept. In the meantime, old Sam Hickey, the gardener, and his stalwart son Jerusah, had been summoned to aid in dragging out one of the aeroplanes.

"We only have two on hand," explained Peggy; "my brother has forwarded the others that we built to Mr. James Bell, the mining man. They are being used in aerial gold transportation across the Nevada desert."

"Indeed! That is most interesting."

Sam Hickey flung open the big doors and revealed the interior of the shed with the two scarab-like monoplanes standing within. A strong smell of gasoline and machine-oil filled the air. The officer glanced at Peggy's dainty figure in astonishment. It seemed hard to associate this refined, exquisite young girl with the rough actualities of machinery and aeroplanes.

But Peggy, with a word of excuse, dived suddenly into a small room. While she was gone, Miss Prescott entertained the young officer with many tales of her harrowing experiences on the Nevada desert. To all of which he listened with keen attention. At least he did so to all outward appearance, but his eyes were riveted on the door through which Peggy had vanished.

When she emerged a very business-like Peggy had taken the place of the lounger in the hammock. A linen duster, fitting tightly, covered her from top to toe. A motoring bonnet of maroon silk imprisoned her hair, and upon its rim, above her forehead, was perched a pair of goggles. Gauntlets encased her hands.

"Looks rather too warm to be comfortable, doesn't it?" she laughed. "But we shall find it cool enough up above."

"Perhaps the lieutenant——" ventured Miss Prescott.

"Oh, yes. How stupid of me not to have thought of it!" exclaimed Peggy. "Mr. Bradbury, you will find aviation togs inside there."

"By Jove; she knows enough not to call a naval officer 'lieutenant,'" thought the young officer, as, with a bow and a word of thanks, he vanished to equip himself for his aerial excursion.

By the time he was invested in a similar long duster, with weighted seams, and had donned a cap and goggles, the larger of the two aeroplanes, named the Golden Butterfly, was ready for its passengers. Old Sam and his son, who had dragged it out—it moved easily on its landing wheels—stood by, their awe of the big craft showing plainly on their faces.

A section of the fence had been made removable, so as to give the Prescott aeroplanes a free run from their stable to the smooth slope of the meadows beyond. This was now removed, and Peggy, followed by the young officer, took her place in the chassis. Peggy made a pretty figure at the steering wheel.

15

"The first improvement I should like to call your attention to," she began, in the most business-like tones she could muster up, "is the self-starter. It works by pneumatic power, and does away with the old-fashioned method of starting an aeroplane by twisting the propeller."

The girl opened a valve connected with a galvanized tank, with a pressure gauge on top, and pulled back a lever. Instantly, a hissing sound filled the air. Then, with a dexterous movement, Peggy threw in the spark and turned on the gasoline which the spark would ignite, thereby causing an explosion in the cylinders. But first the compressed air had started the motor turning over. At the right moment Peggy switched on the power and cut off the air. Instantly there was a roar from the exhausts and blue flames and smoke spouted from the motor. The aeroplane shook violently. It would have made an inexperienced person's teeth chatter. But both the officer and Peggy were sufficiently familiar with aeroplanes for it not to bother them in the least.

"Magnificent!" cried the young officer enthusiastically, as he saw the ease with which the compressed air attachment set the motor to working.

"It will do away with assistants to start the machine," he declared the next instant. "The importance of that in warfare can hardly be overestimated."

Peggy was too busy to reply. So far all had gone splendidly. If only she could carry out the whole test as well!

"Ready?" she asked, flinging back the word over her shoulder to Lieutenant Bradbury.

"All ready!" came in a hearty voice from behind her.

Peggy, with a quick movement, threw in the clutch that started the propeller to whirring.

With a drone like that of a huge night-beetle, or prehistoric thunder-lizard, the machine leaped forward as a race-horse jumps under the raised barrier.

In a blur of blue smoke it skimmed through the gap in the palings. Out upon the smooth meadowland it shot, roaring and smoking terrifically. And then, all at once, the jolting motion of the start ceased. It seemed as if the occupants of the chassis were riding luxuriously over a road paved with the softest of eiderdown. The sensation was delightful, exhilarating.

Peggy shut off the exhaust, turning the explosions of the cylinder into a muffler. In almost complete silence they winged upward. Up, up, toward the fleecy clouds she had been lazily watching, but a short time before, from the hammock.

The Golden Butterfly had never done better.

"You're a darling!" breathed Peggy confidentially to the motor that with steady pulse drove them upward and onward.

CHAPTER IV
IN A STORM

Dwarfed to the merest midgets, the figures about the Prescott house waved enthusiastically, as the golden-winged monoplane made a graceful swoop high above the elms and maples surrounding it. Other figures could be glimpsed too, now, running about excitedly outside the barn-like structure housing the Mortlake aeroplanes.

"Guess they think you are stealing a march on them," drawled Lieut. Bradbury.

A wild, reckless feeling, born of the thrilling sensation of aerial riding, came over Peggy. She would do it—she would. With a scarcely perceptible thrust of her wrist, she altered the angle of the rudder-like tail, and instantly the obedient Golden Butterfly began racing through space toward the Mortlake plant.

The naval officer, quick to guess her plan, laughed as happily as a mischievous boy.

"What a lark!" he exclaimed. "It's contrary to all discipline, but it's jolly good fun."

Peggy turned a small brass-capped valve—the timer. At once the aeroplane showed accelerated speed. It fairly cut through the air. Both the occupants were glad to lower their goggles to protect their eyes from the sharp, cutting sensation of the atmosphere, as they rushed against it—into its teeth, as it were.

Peggy glanced at the indicator. The black pointer on the white dial was creeping up—fifty, sixty, sixty-two—she would show this officer what the Prescott monoplane could do.

"Sixty-four! Great Christmas!"

The exclamation came from the officer. He had leaned forward and scanned the indicator eagerly.

"We'll do better when we have our new type of motor installed," said Peggy, with a confident nod. The young fellow gasped.

"This is the twentieth century with a vengeance," he murmured, sinking back in his rear seat, which was as comfortably upholstered as the luxurious tonneau of a five-thousand-dollar automobile.

Like a darting, pouncing swallow, seeking its food in mid-air, the Golden Butterfly swooped, soared and dived in long, graceful gradients above the Mortlake plant. Once Peggy brought the aeroplane so close to the ground in a long, swinging sweep, that it seemed as if it could never recover enough "way" to rise again. Even the officer, trained in a strict school to repress his emotions, tightened his lips, and then opened them to emit a relieved gasp.

So close to the gaping machinists and the anger-crimsoned Mortlake did the triumphant aeroplane swoop, that Peggy, to her secret amusement could trace the astonished look on the faces of the employees and the chagrined expression that darkened Mortlake's countenance.

"I guess I've given them something to think over," she said mischievously, flinging back a brilliant smile at the dazed young officer.

"Now," she exclaimed the next moment, "for a distance flight. I'm anxious to put the Golden Butterfly through all her paces. Oh, by the way, the balancer. I haven't shown you how that works yet."

If Peggy's bright eyes had not been veiled by goggles, the officer might have seen a mischievous gleam flash into them, like a wind ripple over the placid surface of a blue lake.

Suddenly the aeroplane slanted to one side, as if it must turn over. Peggy had banked it on a sharp aerial curve. The young officer, in spite of himself, in defiance of his training, gave a gasp.

"I say — —"

But the words had hardly left his lips before the aeroplane was back on a level keel once more. At the same time a rasping, sliding sound was heard.

"Like to see how that was done?" asked Peggy, with a bewitching smile.

"Yes. By Jove, I thought we were over for an instant. But how — — "

"That we shall be glad to show you when the United States government has contracted for a number of the Prescott aeroplanes," retorted Peggy.

The young officer bit his lip.

"Confound it," he thought, "is this chit of a girl making fun of me?"

Young officers have a high idea of their own dignity. Mr. Bradbury colored a bit with mortification. But Peggy quickly dispelled his temporary chagrin.

"You see," she explained, "it would never do for us to reveal all our secrets, would it? You agree with me, don't you?"

"Oh, perfectly. You are quite right. Still, I confess that you have aroused all my inquisitiveness."

Peggy being busied just then with a bit of machinery on the bulkhead separating the motor from the body of the chassis, made no reply. But presently, when she looked up, she gave a sharp exclamation.

The sky, as if by magic, had grown suddenly dark. Above the pulsating voice of the motor could be heard the rumble of thunder. All at once a vivid flash of lightning leaped across the horizon. One of those sudden storms of summer had blown up from the sea, and Peggy knew enough of Long Island weather to know that these disturbances were usually accompanied by terrific winds—squalls and gusts that no aeroplane yet built or thought of could hope to cope with.

"We're running into dirty weather, it seems," remarked the officer. "I thought I noticed some thunderheads away off on the horizon when we first went up."

"I wish you'd mentioned them then," said the straightforward Peggy; "as it is, we'll have to descend till this blows over."

"What, won't even the wonderful equalizer render her safe?"

"No, it won't. It will do anything reasonable. But you've no idea of the fury of the wind that comes with these black squalls."

"Indeed I have. Last summer I was off Montauk Point in the Dixie. Something went wrong with the steering gear just as one of these self-same young hurricanes came bustling up. I tell you, it was "all hands and the cook" for a while. It hardly blows much harder in a typhoon."

Peggy gazed below her over the darkening landscape anxiously. There seemed to be trees, trees everywhere, and not a bit of cleared ground. All at once, as they cleared some woods, she spied a bit of meadowland. The hay which had covered it earlier in the summer had been cropped. It afforded an ideal landing-place. But the wind was puffy now, and Peggy did not dare to attempt short descending spirals. Instead, trusting to the balancing device doing its duty faithfully, she swung down in long circles.

Just as they touched the ground with a gentle shock, much minimized, thanks to the shock-absorbers with which the Golden Butterfly was fitted, the storm burst in all its fury. Bolt after bolt of vivid lightning ripped and tore across the darkened sky, which hung like a pall behind the terrific electrical display. The rain came down in torrents.

"Just in time," laughed the young officer, as he aided Peggy in dragging the aeroplane under the shelter of an open cart-shed. It was quite snug and dry once they had it under the roof. A short distance off stood a farm-house of fairly comfortable appearance. Smoke issuing from one of its chimneys showed that it was occupied.

"Let's go over there and see if we can dry our things," suggested Peggy. "I'm wet through."

"Same here," was the laughing reply; "but a sailor doesn't mind that. One actually gets webbed feet in the navy — like ducks, you know."

Ignoring this remarkable contribution to natural history, Peggy gathered up her skirts daintily and fled across the meadow to the farm-house. It was only a few hundred feet, but the rain came down so hard that both she and her escort were wetter than ever by the time they arrived at the door. It was shut, and except for the lazy wisps of smoke issuing from the chimney, there was no sign of life about the place.

The lieutenant knocked thunderously. No answer.

"Try again," said Peggy; "maybe they are in some other part of the house."

"Perhaps they were scared of the aeroplane and have all retired into hiding," suggested Mr. Bradbury.

He rapped again, louder this time, but still no reply.

"They must all be asleep," he said, applying himself once more to a thunderous assault on the door, but to no avail. A silence hung about the place, broken only by the roar and rattle of the thunder.

"It's positively uncanny," shuddered Peggy. "It's like Red Riding Hood and the Three Little Bears."

"One would think that even a bear would open the door on such an occasion as this," said her companion, redoubling his efforts to attract attention. Finally he gave the door handle a twist. It yielded, and the door was speedily found to be unlocked. The officer shoved it open and disclosed a neat farm-house kitchen. In a newly blackened stove, which fairly shone, was a blazing fire. An old clock ticked sturdily in one corner. The floor was scrubbed as white as snow, and on a shelf above the shining stove was an array of gleaming copper pans that gladdened Peggy's housewifely heart.

"What a dear of a place!" she exclaimed. "But where are the folks who own it?"

"Haven't the least idea," said the officer gayly; "but that stove looks inviting to me. Let's get over to it and get dried out a bit. Then we can commence to investigate."

"But, really, you know, we've not the least right in here. Suppose they mistake us for burglars, and shoot us?"

"Not much danger of that. They'd shoot me first, anyhow, because I'm the most burglarious looking of the two. Queer, though, where they all can be."

"It's worse than queer—it's weird. Good gracious!" exclaimed Peggy, as a sudden thought struck her, "suppose there should be trapdoors?"

"Trapdoors!" Her companion was plainly puzzled.

"Yes. You know in most books when two folks run across a deserted farm-house there's always a trapdoor or a ghost or something. Suppose — — Good heavens, what's that?"

From without had come a most peculiar sound. A whirring, like the noise one would suppose would be occasioned by a gigantic locust. Then something—a huge, indefinite shadow—darkened the windows of the farm-house kitchen. Peggy gave a shrill squeal of alarm, while Lieut. Bradbury gallantly ran to the door and flung it open.

CHAPTER V

PEGGY A HEROINE

"It's — it's another aeroplane!" cried the officer, with a shout of amazement.

"What!"

Peggy sprang to her feet.

"A large red one?"

"Yes. Come here and look. They're just running it under the same shed as ours — yours, I mean."

The girl aviator sprang toward the door. Through the rain she peered to where, across the meadow, two dim figures, clad in oilskins, could be seen shoving a big aeroplane under the same shelter that already protected the Golden Butterfly.

"Well, if this isn't the ultimate!" she gasped.

"I beg your pardon?" asked the young man at her side.

"The ultimate! That's my way of expressing what the boys call 'the limit.' Why, that's Jess and Jimsy Bancroft, in their new aeroplane — the one Roy built for them. Well, did you ever! Oh, Jess! Oh, Jimsy!"

Peggy raised her voice and shouted. In response they saw the oil-skinned figures turn, and through the driving downpour came an answering shout. Presently, across the dripping meadows, the two figures began advancing. All this time the lightning was ripping in a manner to make Peggy shield her eyes occasionally. The thunder, too, was terrific, and the earth seemed to vibrate to its rolling detonations.

"Well, Peggy!" gasped Jess, her dark eyes peering from under her waterproof hood, as she and her brother arrived at the threshold of the farm-house, "what on earth does this mean?"

"Yes, give an account of yourself at once," demanded Jimsy. "Roy had us on the phone. Asked if you'd flown in our direction. We said no, but we'd take a flight and look for you. In our enthusiasm, we didn't notice the storm coming up. But luckily, being young persons of forethought, we had oilskins in a locker of the machine, and — — "

"And here we are," finished Jess, shooting a "killing" glance from under her hood at the good-looking young man at Peggy's side.

"Aren't you going to ask us in?" demanded Jimsy the next minute. "For hospitality, I don't think you rate very high. We — — "

"Well, you see, we are here ourselves without knowing if we have any right to be," rejoined Peggy. "But come in and I'll explain. First of all, I want you to meet Mr. Bradbury of the United States Navy. He came to test the Prescott aeroplanes. Mr. Bradbury, this is Miss Bancroft, and her brother — — "

"Jimsy," put in that irrepressible youth. "Glad to meet you, sir. Almost as much at sea here as in mid-Atlantic."

Laughing, they all entered the farm-house kitchen, while Peggy hastily explained the state of affairs there.

"Well, so long as they don't put in an appearance before we get dry, I'm sure I don't care," said Jimsy airily. "What a delightful old kitchen. It might have come out of a picture book."

He and the naval officer were soon deep in conversation, leaving Peggy and Jess alone.

"My dear Peggy," exclaimed Jess, with a smile that showed all her white even teeth, "what will you do next? Don't you think it's a bit — er — er — unconventional for one of the foremost members of Sandy Beach's younger set to be flying about the country with a good-looking young naval officer?"

"Nonsense," retorted Peggy sharply, "as the only representative of the Prescott aeroplanes on the ground, I had to do it. If it hadn't been for this old storm, I'd have been home long ago."

"So should we. What a coincidence we should have met here. Is this—this——"

"Lieutenant," prompted Peggy.

"Is this lieutenant going to stay long in Sandy Beach?"

"Dear me, no. He is only on a flying visit—no pun intended. He was to have taken in the establishment of the Mortlake Aeroplane Company this afternoon. You know, they are in that red, barn-like place, down the road from our place, although Roy and I only found it out to-day."

"That was one of the things I wanted to talk to you about, Peggy dear," said Jess, sinking into an old-fashioned Andrew Jackson chair by the hearth. "Dad said at dinner last night that he had heard in New York that a lot of their stock had been floated on Wall Street, and that that hateful old Mr. Harding was back of it."

"They are actually selling stock?" asked Peggy, growing a bit pale.

"Yes. They have half-page advertisements in a lot of papers, I believe. Dad said so. But why do you look so distressed, Peggy?"

"Because they must be very sure of the merits of their machines, if they are going ahead so confidently."

"Rumor has it that their make of aeroplane is the most up-to-date and complete yet constructed, but nobody knows the details so far. They have kept that part of it close."

"They are making a bid for the navy contracts, at any rate," said Peggy presently, after a pause, during which both girls winked and blinked at the lightning and stared at the red glow of the fire.

"So you said. But you stole a march on them by kidnapping your lieutenant in this way."

"You ought to give the weather credit for that," laughed Peggy, "but seriously, Jess, there is no sentiment in things of this kind. If the Mortlake machine is a better machine than ours, the Mortlake will be the type adopted by the government."

"I suppose that's so," agreed Jess, with a wry face. "But I hate to think of that old Harding creature getting any — — "

The door flew open suddenly, and a tall, thin-faced woman in a raincoat, and holding up an umbrella, stood in the doorway.

"Well, for the land's sake!" she ejaculated, looking fairly dumfounded, as she comprehended the scene and the young folks enjoying the unrequested hospitality of her kitchen.

But the words had hardly left her lips, and she was still standing there, like an image carved from stone, when a fearful light illumined the whole scene. It was followed almost instantaneously by a clap of thunder so deafening that the girls involuntarily quailed before it.

A fiery ball darted from the chimney and sped across the room, exploding in fragments with a terrific noise on the opposite side, just above the heads of Jimsy and Lieut. Bradbury.

Stunned by the shock, they both collapsed in heaps on the floor, while the farm woman's shrieks filled the air. At the same instant, a pungent, sinister odor filled the atmosphere.

"The house is on fire!" shrieked the woman in a frenzied voice.

Smoke rolled down into the room, and the acrid fumes grew sharper.

"The house is on fire, and my baby is up-stairs!"

"Where?" demanded Peggy.

"In the room above this!" groaned the woman, taking a few steps and then fainting.

"Jess," cried Peggy in a tense voice, "take that bucket and get water from that pump in the corner and then follow me."

"But the boys!" gasped Jess.

"They are only stunned. I saw Jimsy's arm move just now, and the lieutenant is breathing."

With these words, she started from the room, darting up a narrow stairway leading from one end of the kitchen to the upper regions.

"What are you going to do?" shouted Jess, her voice shaky with alarm.

"Save that child if I can," flung back Peggy, plunging bravely up the smoke-laden stairway.

In the unfamiliar house, and half blinded and choked by smoke and sulphurous fumes, Peggy had a hard task before her. But she pluckily plunged forward, feeling her way by the walls, and keeping her head low, where the smoke was not so thick. As she reached what she deemed was the top of the staircase, she thought she heard a tiny voice crying out in alarm.

Following the direction of the sounds, she staggered along a hallway and then reeled into an open door. The smoke was not so thick in the room, but its fumes were heavy enough. In a crib in one corner lay a child of about two years of age. Its rose-leaf of a face was wrinkled up in its efforts to make its terrified little voice heard.

Peggy darted upon it and hugged it close to her. Then, with renewed courage, she started to make her way back again. But more smoke than ever was rolling along the passage, and it was a hard task.

"I must do it—I must," Peggy kept saying to herself, clinging the while to the terrified child.

But at the head of the staircase the conditions appalled her. The smoke was thick as a blanket there. Yet plunge through it, Peggy knew she must. Still holding the child tightly, she bravely entered the dense smother, stooping as low as she dared.

But before she had taken more than two steps in the obscurity, a dreadful feeling, as if a hand was at her throat and choking her, overcame the girl.

She tried to call out, but she could not. Her head was reeling, her eyes blinded. All at once something in her head seemed to snap with a loud report. Still clutching her little burden tightly, Peggy plunged forward dizzily — and knew no more.

CHAPTER VI

FARMER GALLOWAY'S "SAFE DEPOSIT"

When she came to herself again, it was in a confusion of voices and sounds of hurrying footsteps. She was lying on a lounge in a stuffy "best" parlor, which smelled as moldy as "best" parlors in farm-houses are wont to do. Bending over her was the angular woman who had entered just as the bolt of lightning, that had caused all the trouble, struck the house.

"Is — is the baby all right?" asked Peggy, as she took in her surroundings.

"Yes, thanks to you, my dear. Oh, how can I ever thank you?" exclaimed the woman, a thrill of real gratitude in her voice. "And the fire is out, too. My husband and his men had been at work in a distant field and were sheltering themselves under a shed. I had just taken some water to them when the storm broke. When they saw the big flash and heard the crash, they knew that something right around the house must have been struck. They ran through the storm as fast as they could, and got here in time to put out the flames."

"And Jess and Jimsy and — —"

"And that other young fellow? Why, they — —"

"Never felt better in their lives," came Jimsy's cheerful voice from the door, which framed, beside himself, Jess, and the young naval officer.

"The first time I was ever knocked out by lightning," declared the latter, "and really it's quite invigorating."

Jess glided across the room to Peggy's side and threw her arms about her neck.

"Oh, Peggy, how brave and good you are!" she exclaimed. "I was dreadfully frightened, when you came plunging down through that smoke. I was just trying to make my way through it with a bucket, when you came toppling down the stairs. I managed to catch you and support you into the kitchen."

"I think some one else is the bravest," smiled Peggy, patting her chum's shoulder. "I'm so glad that the baby wasn't hurt. Poor little thing, it looked so cute in its crib. I remember seizing it up and then the smoke came, and after a few minutes it all got black and — —"

"And all's well that ends well," declared Jimsy, capering about. "We've telephoned to your home to Roy, Peggy, and he'll be over in a short time with an auto."

"But what about the Butterfly?" asked Peggy.

"My dear girl," announced Jimsy, in his most pompous tones, "it would be impossible for you to guide her home this evening. Your nerves would not stand it. See, it's come out quite fine, now, after the storm, and Roy will spin you home in the machine in no time."

"Perhaps that would be best," agreed Peggy. "And I can come out, or Roy can, to-morrow, and get the aeroplane — that is," she added, turning to the farm woman, "if it won't be in your way."

"If you had a thousand of them air-buggies around here, miss, they wouldn't be in our way," came in a hearty, gruff tone from the door. They looked up to see a big farmer-like looking person, with a fringe of black whiskers running under his chin in a half-moon, standing there.

"This is my husband, Isaac Galloway," said the woman, introducing the owner of the farm.

"At your service, gents and ladies," said the farmer. "What that young woman did fer us ter-day ther' ain't no way of repaying; but anything Ike Galloway kin do any time ye kin count on him fer."

He moved toward an object they had not previously noticed, an iron door in the wall. Turning a knob this way and that, he presently flung it open, revealing the inside of a wall safe. Thrusting his hand inside, he drew out a bundle of bills. Then, closing the door again, and adjusting the combination, he said:

"Jes' goin' ter give ther boys a bit of thank you fer helpin' me put out ther fire. If any of you folks would like — —"

"Oh, no. No, thank you," laughed Peggy, sitting up and feeling, except for a slight dizziness, almost herself again.

"Very well; no harm meant," said the farmer, as he shuffled out of the room and into the kitchen, where he distributed his largess.

"Quite an idea," commented Jimsy, regarding the wall safe. "I suppose you have quite a lot of money on hand at times, and it is safest to keep it so," he added, addressing the farmer's wife.

"Yep," was the rejoinder; "Ike got his money fer his corn crop ther other day — two thousand dollars, what with ther corn and ther early apples. It's all in thar, except what he's jes' took out."

"Aren't you afraid of burglars coming and blowing the door of the safe off?" asked Peggy.

"Lands sakes, no. We'd hear 'em. Besides, that's a patent safe, an' if it is opened without a knowledge of the combination, it would take a plaguey long time to do."

Just then the farmer came back, and after some more general conversation the whir of an approaching automobile announced the arrival of Roy. The lad was naturally much interested in the doings of the afternoon, as excitedly related to him by everybody at once, and was favorably impressed with the young naval officer. Of course, he did not ask him his opinion of the Prescott aeroplane, but from remarks Lieut. Bradbury dropped, Roy gathered that he was much pleased with its performance.

Soon afterward Jess and Jimsy shot skyward, in the now still air, in their red aeroplane — the Red Dragon Fly, as it had been christened, and amid warm farewells from the farmer and his wife, the auto buzzed off.

They had traversed a mile or more, when, on rounding a corner at a narrow part of the road, they came almost head-on against another machine coming in the opposite direction.

Both cars were compelled to slow down, so that the occupants had a good view of each other. Both Roy and Peggy were considerably astonished to see that the oncoming auto was occupied by old Mr. Harding, and that by his side was seated none other than the blue-chinned man, known as Eugene Mortlake.

"Where can they be going?" wondered Roy, as old man Harding favored them with a scowl in passing, and then both cars resumed their normal speed.

"I noticed that this is a private road leading only to that farm," rejoined Peggy; "the right-of-way ends there."

"Then that must be their destination, for there are no other houses on this road."

"Looks that way," assented Roy. "Queer, isn't it?"

"Very," responded Peggy. For some inexplicable reason, as the girl spoke, a chill ran through her. She felt a dull sense of foreboding. But the next minute she shook it off. After all, why shouldn't Mr. Harding and Mortlake be driving to the farm? Mr. Harding's financial dealings comprised mortgages in every part of the island. It was quite probable that the farmer was in some way involved in the old man's nets. Possibly that was the reason of all that money being stored in the wall safe.

Refusing courteously an invitation extended by Miss Prescott to spend the night at the homestead, Lieut. Bradbury was driven to the station by Roy, after they had dropped Peggy, and just managed to make a New York train.

"I shall be back to-morrow," he said, "and have a look at Mortlake's machines. Of course, the government wants to give everybody a fair field and no favors."

"Oh, of course," assented Roy, pondering in his own mind what sort of a machine this mysterious Mortlake craft was.

Suddenly there flashed across his mind a thought that had not occurred to him hitherto. The Golden Butterfly had been left under the shed at the farm. What was there to prevent Harding and Mortlake from examining it and acquainting themselves with the intricacies of the self-starting mechanism and the automatic balancing device?

There was no question that the farm must have been their destination. Roy blamed himself bitterly for not foreseeing this. He had half a mind to return to the farm and bring the aeroplane home himself. But it was growing dark, and a distant rumble seemed to presage the return of the afternoon's storm.

"Anyhow," the boy thought, and the thought consoled him, "all those devices are covered by patents, and even if they wanted to, they could not steal them. And yet—and yet——"

But the storm came up sharper than ever that evening, and even had he wished to, Roy would have found it impossible to handle the aeroplane alone in the heavy wind that came now in puffs and now in a steady gale. So Roy put his tiresome thoughts out of his head. But he resolved to get the aeroplane the first thing the following morning.

CHAPTER VII

A CASE FOR THE AUTHORITIES

It was just after breakfast the next morning that a big automobile skimmed past the Prescott home. Peggy and Roy saw it from the windows.

"Why, that's Sheriff Lawley," exclaimed Peggy. "And look, old Mr. Harding is with him, and that Mortlake man."

"That's right. Wonder where they can be going?" said Roy, sauntering out to the garage at the back of the house and giving the matter little more thought. It had been arranged that he was to bring the aeroplane back that morning, driving over with Peggy, Jimsy and Jess in the car, and skimming home in the Butterfly while a part of the party brought the car back. They were to call for Jess and Jimsy at their home, a fine residence overlooking the Sound from a lofty hill.

Jess and Jimsy were waiting for them, and, almost before the car had stopped, they were at its side.

"Heard the news?" asked Jimsy breathlessly.

"No. What is it?" demanded Peggy eagerly.

"Why, that safe at the farm-house was robbed last night. All the money was taken, and they have no clue to the thief."

"How did you hear of it?" asked Roy incredulously. Peggy had told him of the queer wall safe.

"The 'central' told one of the servants and she told Jess. Strange, isn't it?"

"It is odd," agreed Roy. "But if people will keep their money in such places, it is hardly surprising if they lose it. Did you hear any details?"

"No, but no doubt we shall when we reach the farm-house," put in Jess; "isn't it thrilling, though?"

"Not very thrilling for poor Galloway, who lost the money," said Peggy. "I expect he didn't make it any too easily."

On their arrival at the Galloway farm-house, the young people found a scene of great excitement. The sheriff, red-faced and important, was examining several farm hands beneath one of the big elms, while in the background stood the farmer and his wife, looking somewhat perplexed, as well as worried.

As the Prescott auto drove up, old Mr. Harding, in his usual rusty black suit, rose from his seat under the elm, and whispered something to the sheriff. The blue-chinned, thick-necked Mortlake arose also. All three turned and gazed curiously at the young occupants of the car, as it slowed down.

"Good morning, Mr. and Mrs. Galloway," cried Peggy. "We were dreadfully sorry to hear of your loss. Have you any clue yet?"

There was something curiously cold in the woman's voice, as she replied in the negative. Her husband looked sullen and merely nodded. The sheriff now rose and came toward the machine. He knew all the young folks and greeted them briefly. At his heels pressed old Harding and his companion. They whispered in the sheriff's ear as he advanced, and seemed to be urging him to something.

"I understand that you folks was in this house yesterday afternoon?" began the sheriff abruptly.

"Why, yes, during the storm," said Peggy. "There was Lieut. Bradbury, of the United States Navy — —"

Harding and Mortlake exchanged annoyed glances. This was confirmation of their fears.

"Yes, go on," urged the sheriff.

"And myself, and Mr. Bancroft here and his sister, and later my brother came."

"Do you recall the safe being opened while you were in the room? I presume from the remark you made when you drove up that you know of the robbery."

"We heard of it at the Bancroft's, but we don't know the details."

"That is not necessary. Answer my questions, please. Who was in the parlor beside yourself when Mr. Galloway opened the wall safe to reward the men who had helped him extinguish the fire?"

"Why, Jimsy—I mean Mr. Bancroft—his sister and Lieut. Bradbury, beside, of course, Mr. and Mrs. Galloway."

"What! Your brother was not there?"

"Certainly not. He didn't come till later."

"Then your brother didn't see the safe opened?"

"Of course not," struck in Roy. "I was here only a very brief time. But what does all this mean? I don't understand."

"It means that you are cleared of a grave suspicion," said the sheriff. "Mr. Harding and Mrs. Galloway's brother, Mr. Mortlake, here——"

"Her brother!" exclaimed Peggy in an undertone.

The sheriff went on:

"Seemed to have an idea that Roy Prescott was here at the time. They even went so far as to intimate that——"

But old Mr. Harding was tugging frantically at the sheriff's arm. He was seconded by Mortlake. Interpreting the signals aright, he stopped short.

"In fact, it looked suspicious," he concluded lamely. He turned and went off, followed by Harding and Mortlake.

"How did you ever come to make such a mistake?" snarled old Harding, as they walked away much crestfallen, "we haven't a leg to stand on, now."

"Why, confound it all," retorted Mortlake, "my sister mentioned a young man being with the girl in the aeroplane, and I took it for granted that it was her brother."

"And a nice mess you've got us both into, with your 'taking it for granted,'" snorted the old miserly financier of Sandy Beach. "It looks as if we'd got ourselves in a trap now."

"Nonsense. Who's to know we have the money? I'll take the first opportunity to send it back, and no more will be heard of the matter. Lucky I didn't hide it in his aeroplane, as I intended to do."

"Yes; but we've still got the cub as our rival. I wish I could think of some plan to choke him off. That scheme of yours to blame the robbery on him would have been all right if you'd only made sure of your facts first."

"Don't worry. Our chance will come yet. I'll make that whole outfit regret bitterly that they ever stole a march on us by kidnapping that officer."

"To have discredited him with the navy would have been the best way, however," said old Harding brusquely.

"I'll find a way to do that yet," Mortlake promised.

In the meantime, speculation and wonder had ruled among the occupants of Roy's auto. Everything seemed very much muddled, but one fact stood out clearly, and that was that an attempt had been made to cast suspicion, if not the actual guilt of the robbery, upon Roy.

For what object?

"I have it," cried Peggy suddenly. "If they could have placed Roy under a cloud of suspicion, it would have worked to his discredit with the naval authorities, and might have resulted in our aeroplane being denied a place in the trials. That seems plain enough."

They all agreed that it did. But Jimsy said suddenly: "If that was the case, why didn't they try to make out that I stole it?"

"Because—forgive me Jimsy—you're not Roy. Without him, the tests of the Prescott aeroplane could hardly be conducted. Unless——"

"Unless a certain young person named Peggy Prescott undertook to take charge of them," cried Jess loyally.

"Don't be foolish, Jess," warned Peggy; "but look, here is Mrs. Galloway coming to speak to us."

The farmer's wife approached the automobile, from which none of the party had as yet alighted. She was followed by her husband. Both began apologizing profusely for the questions of the sheriff.

"But land's sakes alive," exclaimed the farmer's wife, "I declar ter goodness, we've bin so flustered thet I don' know no more than a wet hen. My brother, that's Mr. Mortlake, was dead sot on it bein' one of you folks, but I knew that was reediculous."

They hardly knew whether to be angry or to laugh at the woman's blunt frankness. But Roy struck in with a question:

"Wasn't Mr. Mortlake, accompanied by Harding, out here last night?"

"Why, yes," said the woman, with perfect candor. "They stayed quite a while. Harding hed some business with Ike, an'——"

"An' Gene Mortlake said he'd like ter hev a look at yer aeroplane. Yer know he's in thet thar business hisself," volunteered Ike confidentially.

Peggy felt as if she could have groaned aloud. Roy's fears, earlier confided to her, seemed to have been based on a true presentiment. The blue-jowled Mortlake had undoubtedly improved his opportunity to study the Golden Butterfly at close range. The farmer's next words confirmed her.

"Reckon he was powerful interested, too," the farmer went on, "fer he made a lot uv ther nicest droorings you ever seen, an'—why, what's the trouble?"

For Roy, hardly knowing what he intended to do, had jumped from the machine and was sprinting toward the Harding car. But, as he neared it, the old financier, who with Mortlake was already seated in the tonneau, spoke a word in the chauffeur's ear, and the machine dashed off, leaving Roy enraged and nonplussed.

"Too bad, Roy," breathed Peggy, as, rather crestfallen, the lad returned.

"Oh, I don't know, Sis. Even if they hadn't sneaked off like that, and I'd caught the machine, I guess I'd have been like the dog that chased the train. I wouldn't have known what to do with it when I got it."

"But Roy, their flight confirms their guilt!"

"I know, Sis, but what possible way have we to prove it? The rascals have covered up their tracks cleverly."

A sudden thought struck Peggy, and she turned to the farmer.

"Did any of those bills have an identifying mark on it?" she asked.

The farmer shook his head. But Mrs. Galloway had a better memory.

"Why, yes, Ike," she exclaimed; "that twenty-dollar-bill you got frum Si. Giddens fer ther Baldwins. I re'klect thet it hed a big round O in red ink marked on ther back uv it. It was a bit rubbed out, an' hard ter see, but ef you knew it wuz thar an' luked fer it, you could see it plain enough."

After inquiring about the baby, whose thankful mother declared it to be as well as ever, Roy and Jimsy dragged out the Golden Butterfly and boarded it. It had been arranged that the two girls were to spin back to town in the car, the aeroplane following them as closely as possible from above.

As they chugged out of the farm-yard gate and on to the rough road, Peggy's thoughts kept time to the rhythmic pulsations of the motor:

"A-twenty-dollar-bill-with-a-red-round-O. A-twenty-dollar-bill-with-a-red-round-O."

CHAPTER VIII

MR MORTLAKE LOSES SOME DRAWINGS

Dashing along the rough country road, with every sense on the alert, Peggy found mental occupation enough to drive gloomier thoughts from her mind. The Prescott's car was a good one, with a powerful, sixty-horse motor, and splendidly upholstered. It was painted a dark blue, and was known in the surrounding country as "The Blue Bird." It had been purchased with the money made by the brother and sister from their shares in James Bell's desert mine.

Far above them sailed the aeroplane, its two occupants from time to time waving at their pretty sisters below. But in the upper-air currents, it would have been dangerous to drive at a pace slow enough to keep level with the automobile, and so the aeroplane soon dashed on ahead. From time to time, however, it made circles and swoops, which brought it sometimes in seemingly dangerous closeness to the tree-tops.

All at once Peggy stopped the automobile with a jerk which almost threw Jess, who was unprepared for the shock, out of the car.

"Good gracious, Peggy, what are you trying to do?" she gasped.

"Look!" cried Peggy, pointing with wide eyes.

In the center of the road lay a rolled-up bundle of papers secured with a rubber band.

"Somebody has dropped something from another auto or a wagon," cried Jess.

"I think so," said Peggy in excited tones, as she descended from the car, "and I've an idea that these papers have been dropped from Mr. Harding's car. It must have been the only one to pass here recently, as this road runs direct to the farm and nowhere else."

She stooped down in the road and picked up the bundle and then, with a beating heart, she opened it. But for an inward intuition of what its contents would prove to be, Peggy, with her rigid ideas of honor, could not have brought herself to do this. As her eyes fell on the first sheet, and she saw that it was covered with annotations and sketches, she gave a little cry.

"Oh, Jess! The luck! The wonderful, wonderful luck!"

"Why, what is it? A bundle of thousand-dollar bills, or — — "

"It isn't that or anything," cried Peggy; "it's — oh, Jess — it's the sketches and plans of our aeroplane that Mortlake and his accomplice Harding were spiriting away."

"They must have dropped them from their automobile," said Jess.

"Or, more likely, from the pockets of one of them. See, the ground is trampled about here. It looks to me as if they had had a break-down, and were fixing it when the papers fell out and were left behind unnoticed. Oh, what a bit of luck! If they had had those papers, it would have meant — — "

A shrill cry from Jess interrupted her. At the same moment Peggy became conscious of a presence behind her. She wheeled sharply and found herself facing two bloated-faced individuals, one of whom carried a heavy cudgel. Their clothes and broken boots, and their leering, odious appearance at once proclaimed them of the genus tramp.

"Waal!" growled one of the men, with an ugly leer, "we didn't hardly expec' ter run inter such luck ez this. Foun' suthin' vallerable, hev yer? Reckin' it must hev bin dropped by that auto that jes' went round the corner beyond. We'll hev ter trouble you for it, miss."

He held out a filthy hand, while Peggy, with a beating heart, fell back toward the car.

"Frum what we hearn' yer sayin', I guess the papers is vallerable, all right," chimed in the first speaker's companion. "Come on, now. Fork over. You know it ain't honest ter take wot don't berlong ter ye, an' by yer own confession them papers don't."

"What right have you to demand them?" asked Peggy boldly enough, despite her inward terror; "you had better go on at once, or— —"

"Waal, or what?" sneered the other. "We've got ye here on a lonely road. You can't escape us. Come on, hand over them papers. We'll see that ther rightful owners git 'em, and that we git er reward beside. See?"

Peggy's reply was to leap nimbly into the machine. But to her horror the two tramps followed instantly. Jess cowered back in her seat. Her pale lips moved, but she said nothing.

"Tell yer wot," burst out the man with the club, "you gals give us ten bones a piece—the money don't mean much to folks like you—an' we'll let yer go. If not— —"

A sudden inspiration came to Peggy—a flash of recollection.

"Why didn't you say that before?" she said cheerfully. "I'll be glad to give you the money. Wait a minute while I get it out."

She raised the cushion of the front "bucket seat," and dived beneath it with one hand. The men watched her with greedy, yet suspicious eyes.

"Ain't tryin' ter fool us, are yer?" growled one of them, "'cos ef you air— —"

He raised his club threateningly, just as Peggy's hand withdrew from beneath the cushion. Something bright flashed in it.

"Look out, Mike. She's got a gun!" shouted one of the men, falling back.

The other whipped a hand amidst his rags and was just about to aim a pistol, when:

"Phiz-z-z-z-z-z-z!"

From the shiny object Peggy held in her hand, a fine stream of some sort of liquid jetted forcibly.

The fellow with the gun threw his hands up to his face, and dropping the pistol, staggered back with a howl of agony. The other darted off without even looking at him. The air was filled with a pungent scent of ammonia, and a quiet smile of triumph curled Peggy's red lips as she started the car in motion once more.

"Oh, Peggy, how brave you are!" gasped Jess. "Whatever was that you used? I hope the poor man isn't badly hurt, although he was so horrid."

"I just remembered in time, Jess dear," said Peggy, as she sped the car along, "that we had under the seat an ammonia pistol for use on vicious dogs. I used it on another sort of a dog, that's all, and it proved equally effective."

Just at this moment Peggy turned out to avoid another car that was approaching them from the opposite direction. In a second she saw that it carried Harding and Mortlake. They both looked angry and blank. Peggy guessed at once that they had discovered their loss. But she resolved not to stop unless they did and asked questions. She felt that such a despicable act as they had attempted to perpetrate deserved no help on her part.

"Hey, there!" shouted old Mr. Harding, as his car was slowed down by the chauffeur. "Hey, stop! I want to speak to you!"

"He's polite about it, isn't he?" whispered Jess. "Are you going to tell him, Peggy?"

"Cer-tain-ly not," rejoined Peggy, with a tightening of her lips. "Why should I? He tried to fasten a theft on my brother this morning, and then caps the climax by instigating Mortlake to try to steal the ideas of our aeroplane."

"Hey, girls, seen a package on the road?" bawled old Mr. Harding, as Peggy slowed up and stopped.

"I recovered some of my own property, if that is what you mean," said Peggy slowly, a dull flush rising to her cheeks.

"Well—well! What d'ye mean by that, hey? What d'ye mean by that?"

"You may construe it any way you wish to, Mr. Harding," was the cold rejoinder, and to avoid further questioning, Peggy sped up her machine, and soon vanished in a cloud of dust.

The old financier turned to his companion with a look of disgusted amazement.

"What d'ye think of that, hey, Mortlake?" he snapped out. "What d'ye think of that? Fine young girls, eh? Nice products of the twentieth century, hey?"

"Oh, let's get on and see if we can't find that roll of papers somewhere along here," rejoined Mortlake impatiently. "I don't think it's likely they could have seen it. It must have fallen from my pocket where the car broke down and I got out."

"Hey? Oh, yes, yes. That's it. Drive on, Tom. Drive us to where the car broke down."

In a few seconds they reached the spot just in time to see the two tramps who had molested the girls making off.

"There they go!" shouted Mortlake, "those fellows must have found them. I wouldn't lose those sketches for a thousand dollars. Put on more speed, Tom, and overtake them."

The chauffeur did as he was bid, and the car leaped ahead. In a few chugs it had reached the tramps' side, they having stopped, bewildered, in the meantime.

"Why, blow me, Bill," said one to the other, as the car came up, "if it ain't the self-same gents as drove down the road a while ago."

"Give me those papers, you rascals!" shouted Mortlake, almost flinging himself out of the car, "give them to me or— —"

"Hold your horses, guv'ner! Hold your hosses," counseled the hobo who had received the dose of ammonia, and whose eyes were still red from its effects.

"Wot papers might you be lookin' fer?" asked this fellow cautiously, although he knew very well.

"A bundle of papers I dropped," panted Mortlake. "Didn't you find them."

"Naw!" grunted the red-eyed tramp.

"Naw!" echoed the other.

"Be careful what you say. If you are lying, it will go hard with you."

The warning came from old Mr. Harding.

"We know that, guv'ner. But we ain't got 'em. Search us, if yer like."

The knights of the road spread their arms to signify their willingness to be searched. Mortlake groaned. It was evident that neither of the tatterdermalions had the papers. But what had become of them? In his distress and chagrin, Mortlake gave an audible groan.

This the tramps seemed to construe as a favorable sign. One winked to the other, and the red-eyed one spoke.

"Wots it worth if we tell yer where them papers are, guv'ners both?"

"What, you know!" cried Mortlake, while old Mr. Harding spluttered:

"Eh, eh? Hey, what's all this? What's all this?"

"I didn't say we knew," was the cunning reply. "I said what's it worth if we did know."

Mortlake drew out a yellow-backed bill.

"Is this enough?" he asked.

The tramps' eyes rounded as they gazed at the figure.

"Perfec'ly satisfactory, guv'ner," said red eyes.

"Well, where are those papers, then?" snapped Mortlake impatiently.

"Thet thar purty gal wot jest went by in an autermobubble has 'em."

"What!"

"Yes. We saw her pick them up out of the road. We tried to convince her it was dishonest to keep 'em, but she wouldn't listen to us."

"You've done well, and seem to be bright fellows," said Mortlake, handing over the bill to red eyes, who seemed to be the leader of the two, "by the way, you don't belong about here, do you?"

"Oh, no, guv'ner. Our homes is whar we hangs our hats. My permanent address is care of the 'dicky birds.'"

"Well, I may have some work for you to do— —"

"Work, guv'ner? Work's only for the workmen."

"I know all that, but this work is on your own line. I'll pay well, too. If you want to talk it over, come to the Mortlake Aeroplane Factory, outside Sandy Beach at ten o'clock to-night. I'll be there to meet you."

"All right, guv'ner; we'll be, thar. Till then we'll bid yer 'oliver oil,' as ther French say. Come on, Joey."

The worthy pair shuffled off up the road, while Mortlake turned to Harding with a shrug.

"There are two tools made to our hand. We may find them very useful."

"I agree with you," was the dry and rasping reply; "at least, they have put us in possession of one valuable bit of knowledge, hey?"

CHAPTER IX

THE FLIGHT OF THE "SILVER COBWEB"

A week rolled slowly by. A week of suspense, during which they had one or two calls from Lieut. Bradbury, who had been busy down at the Mortlake plant. But the officer was naturally noncommittal concerning his opinion of the comparative merits of the two types of aeroplanes. Equally naturally, of course, the young Prescotts had not questioned him concerning them.

But during this week they had had a glimpse of the Mortlake machine in flight. One still, breathless morning, the air had been filled, soon after dawn, with a vibrant buzzing sound, which Peggy's trained ear had recognized as the song of an aeroplane engine.

She hastened to her brother's room and rapped upon the door. In reply to his sleepy query, the girl rapidly told him of what she had heard. Roy's window faced on the road, and a glance satisfied him that the Mortlake machine was to have its first try-out. Hastily as he dressed, however, he found that Peggy was before him on the dewy lawn, field glasses in hand.

Down the road could be seen, in front of the Mortlake plant, a small crowd of mechanics with one or two dominant figures moving among them. With the glasses, they had no difficulty in making out Mortlake's heavy-shouldered figure, and the slender, upright form of Lieut. Bradbury. All at once the group opened up a bit and they saw a silvery, glittering aeroplane, agleam with new aluminum paint, throbbing and vibrating, as if anxious to be off. Blue smoke eddied up as the motor roared and whirred. The air seemed to vibrate under the sound as if a battery of gatling guns had been discharged.

Fascinated, brother and sister watched the spectacle intently. They saw Mortlake clamber heavily into the machine, followed by Lieut. Bradbury. A mechanic started for the front of the plane and began swinging the propeller.

"At least they haven't cribbed our self-starting device," exclaimed Peggy, as she saw.

The next instant the propeller became a whirring blur, and the aeroplane, after a brief preliminary run, began to climb upward. The morning sun caught its silvered planes and turned them to gold. It was a beautiful and inspiring sight. Even with all that lay at stake, Peggy and Roy could not deny the machine a meed of praise. It was fairy-like in its delicacy of construction, and speedy as a flash.

Thundering like an express train, it dashed above the Prescott home, leaving in its wake the pungent odor of burning castor-oil—the most suitable lubricant for aeroplanes.

Then suddenly—as if a recollection of Peggy's mischievous flight of a few days previously had occurred to him—Mortlake swung the delicate silvery machine about and dashed straight down at the boy and girl standing by the garden gate. So close to their heads did he skim in his desire to show off, that he almost came too low. For one instant it looked as if the machine would be dashed to a premature end, but it recovered buoyancy like a keeled-over racing yacht, and tore upward into the sky at an increased speed.

"Let's get out the Golden Butterfly and follow the——"

"Silver Cobweb!" cried Roy, the name occurring to him in a flash of inspiration as he watched the filmy outlines of the other aeroplane melt in the distance.

"Oh, Roy, what a pretty name."

"Isn't it? But somehow, I like Golden Butterfly best. Our machine may be a bit heavier, but solidity counts in hard service."

Scarcely ten minutes later, and while Mortlake's mechanics and assistants were still craning their necks skyward, another aeroplane, a yellow adventurer of the skies, thundered upward. Not to be outdone by Mortlake, Roy, who was at the wheel, swooped above the rival crowd.

They did not take it with a good grace. Remarks, of which they could not catch the wording, but only the menacing intonation, were hurled upward at them. They received them with a laugh and a wave of the hand, which did not put the Mortlake crowd into any better humor. And then, with a graceful, swinging curve, that banked the machine almost on its beam ends, they were up, off and away in pursuit of the Silver Cobweb, which, by this time, was a mere shoe-button of a dot on the horizon.

"Do you think we can overhaul her, Roy?" ventured Peggy, as they raced through the air, the fresh breath of morning coming refreshingly in their faces.

"Not a chance," admitted Roy cheerfully, "but they'll turn after a while, I guess, and then we'll try the Butterfly against the Cobweb."

But they kept on and on unrelentingly, and still there was no sign of diminution of speed on the part of the Silver Cobweb. Nor did the other aircraft give any indication that she was preparing to put about.

Below them, farms, meadows, villages and crowds of wondering country folk swam by in an ever-changing panorama. The earth beneath them looked like a big saucer divided up into brown, red and green squares, with tiny fly-like dots running and walking about.

All at once Roy gave a shout and pointed. Dead ahead, and not more than a few miles distant, lay a silvery, gleaming streak.

"The sea!"

The exclamation came simultaneously from Peggy and Roy.

They had been traveling due south across the island, and now the broad Atlantic lay stretched beyond the land, shimmering in the sunlight. Far off, they could make out the black smoke of a steamer, hovering above the ocean.

"A mail boat, making for New York," announced Roy.

So fast were they traveling that by this time they could plainly make out the ocean, which, from a silvery streak, was now changed into a dark-blue rolling expanse of salt water.

And still the Silver Cobweb kept on, and gave no sign of turning. Nor, for that matter, had her speed diminished appreciably. The rival aeroplane was now skimming above the water at a height of about a thousand feet. The Golden Butterfly maintained about the same altitude, but the gap between the two aerial craft was not closing up.

"Mortlake's taking a desperate chance to show Lieut. Bradbury what the Cobweb can do," exclaimed Roy. "With a new engine, he's risking too much."

"I guess he's seen us and means to beat us out at all hazards," conjectured Peggy.

And she was right. Mortlake, glancing back a short time before the sea appeared on the horizon, had seen the other aeroplane, and guessing at once what its appearance meant, had determined to keep on, even at the risk of plunging himself and his passenger into the sea.

That was Mortlake's character; he was a man who could brook no rivalry. Used all his life to sweep obstacles aside, he would rather have terminated his career than permit any one to pass him in the race for first place, no matter in what line that first place might lie.

"Are you going to keep on, Roy?"

The question came as a strip of white beach flashed beneath them, and Peggy, peering over the edge of the chassis, saw the big Atlantic swells rolling below them. The thunder of the surf on the beach came clearly to their ears, even at that height.

"What do you think, Sis? We've got lots of gasoline. The motor is working without a hitch. I'd hate to turn back now, particularly with that officer's eyes upon us, as in all probability they are."

"Oh, let's keep on," exclaimed Peggy, casting prudence to the winds. "I feel like you, Roy. If we turn back now, it would look as if we were afraid to trust the Butterfly above the ocean, and, after all, it is a naval contest that we hope to be elected for."

"Forward it is, then," cried Roy exultingly. The tang of the salt wind, the inspiration of the ocean, had come to him. He felt like a corsair—a very modern corsair—urging his craft above the ancient sea.

The vessel, whose smoke they had espied at a distance, was quite close to them now. A huge, black hull, with white passenger decks, rising tier on tier, four huge red funnels with black tops, and slender masts, between which hung the spider-web aerials of her wireless apparatus. Her bow was creaming up the ocean into foam, as she rushed onward at a twenty-four knot gait.

Roy, obeying a daring impulse, let the Golden Butterfly descend. Now they could see her promenade decks lined with white faces peering upward. Here and there the sun glinted on the bright metal work of cameras, all aimed at the wonderful spectacle of the soaring, buoyant Golden Butterfly.

"Oh, if only we could drop a message on her decks!" breathed Peggy eagerly. "I do wish we had a post-card or something— —"

"By ginger," cried Roy suddenly, "I do believe I've got some in my coat-pocket. I bought some in the village yesterday to mail to the chaps back at school. Yes. Here they are, and here's a fountain-pen. Now write all you want."

Peggy took the cards her brother handed to her with his free hand, and, with the fountain-pen, sat down to compose some messages. After a few seconds' thought, she began to write busily. Card after card was covered with her neat penmanship. All this time Roy had kept the Golden Butterflyhovering above the liner, from time to time taking swoops and dives around it like some monstrous sea gull.

Suddenly, from the liner's whistle, a great cascade of white steam spouted.

"Wough-h-h-h-h-h-h-h-h!"

It was the vessel's siren blowing a greeting to the young adventurers of the air. At the same instant a deep-throated roar, a cheer from cabin and steerage passengers alike, winged its way upward. Roy acknowledged it by a graceful wave of his cap. Then the cheering broke forth afresh.

The passengers of the newest ocean giant, the Ruritania, realized that they were seeing a spectacle that would remain in their memories all their lives. Having conquered old ocean with leviathan vessels, man was now seeking to subdue the air to his utility.

CHAPTER X

AN AERIAL POST OFFICE

Peggy addressed half a dozen cards. Two, of course, went to Jess and Jimsy, another to Aunt Sallie Prescott; one to the captain of the Ruritania, and one other, which bore the address, "Eugene Mortlake, Esq."

It was a mischievous freak that made Peggy write this last missive, which read:

TO MR. EUGENE MORTLAKE,

Per Steamer Ruritania — in Mid-air:

Greetings from aeroplane Golden Butterfly.

R. & M. PRESCOTT.

That was all, but Peggy knew that it would serve its prankish purpose.

All this time the Silver Cobweb had been out at sea, but now, apparently detecting the maneuvers of the Golden Butterfly, she headed about, and came racing back. Peggy deftly attached weights — spare bolts from the tool locker — to each of the cards, and then, snatching up a megaphone, she hailed the uniformed figures on the bridge of the great vessel below them.

"Will you be good enough to mail some letters for us?"

"With pleasure!" came the reply in a big, bellowing British voice, from one of the stalwart figures beneath.

"All right; Roy, come down as low as you dare," cried Peggy, catching her bundle of "mail."

Roy threw over a couple of levers and turned a valve. Instantly the Golden Butterfly began to drop in long, beautiful arc. She shot by above the liner's bridge at a height of not more than fifteen feet. At the correct moment Peggy dropped the weighted bundle overboard, and had the satisfaction of seeing one of the officers catch it. The gallant officers, now realizing for the first time that a girl—and a pretty one—was one of the passengers of the big aeroplane, waved their hats and bowed profoundly.

And Peggy—what would Aunt Sallie have said!--Peggy blew them a kiss. But then, as she told Jess later:

"I was in an aeroplane, my dear—a sort of an unattainable possibility, in fact."

In the meantime, Mortlake, in the Silver Cobweb, had been duly mystified as to what the Golden Butterfly was about when she swooped downward on the steamer. For one instant the thought flashed across him that they were disabled. An unholy glee filled him at the thought. If only theGolden Butterfly were to come to grief right under Lieut. Bradbury's eyes, it would be a great feather in the cap of the Mortlake-Harding machine.

But, to his chagrin, he saw them rise the next instant, as cleverly as ever. Lieut. Bradbury, who had been watching the maneuver of the Golden Butterfly, gave an admiring gasp, as he witnessed the daring feat.

"Good heavens!" he exclaimed, and the evident note of astonishment and appreciation in his tones did not tend to increase Mortlake's self-satisfaction.

"The pesky brats," he muttered to himself; "we've got to do something to put them out of the race. There isn't another American-built aeroplane that I fear except that bothersome kids' machine."

And there and then Mortlake began to hatch up a scheme that in the near future was to come very nearly proving disastrous to Peggy and Roy and their high hopes.

"Magnificently handled, don't you think so, Mortlake?" inquired the naval officer, the next instant.

"Yes, very clever," agreed Mortlake, far too smart to show his inward feelings, or to wear his heart upon his sleeve; "very neat. But I can do the same thing if you'd care to see it?"

The naval officer glanced at the puffy features of his companion and his thick, bull-like neck.

"No, thanks," he said. "I've got to be getting back. There's another type of machine I've got to look over out at Mineola. It is really necessary that I reach there as quickly as possible."

"Very well," said Mortlake, inwardly relieved, as he didn't much fancy duplicating Roy's feat, "we'll head straight on for the shore."

"If you please."

But what was the Golden Butterfly doing? As the steamer raced onward, that aerial wonder had swung in a spiral, and was now seemingly hovering about, awaiting the arrival of the Silver Cobweb.

As the two aeroplanes drew abreast, Mortlake muttered something, and bent over his engines. The Cobweb leaped forward like an unleashed greyhound. But the Golden Butterfly was close on her heels, and making almost as good time. Mortlake plunged his hands in among the machinery and readjusted the air valve of the carburetor. Another increase of speed resulted. The indicator crawled up to sixty-six, sixty-eight and then to seventy miles an hour.

"Pressing her a bit, aren't you?" asked the officer, as they seemed to hurtle through the air, so fast did they rush onward.

"Oh, no. She's built for speed," responded Mortlake, with a gratified grin; "she'll leave any such old lumber wagon as that Prescott machine miles behind her any day in the week."

This seemed to be true. The Golden Butterfly, making about sixty miles, was being rapidly left behind.

"I should think you'd be afraid of overheating your cylinders," volunteered the lieutenant.

Now, this was just what Mortlake was afraid of. But, as has been said, he was the sort of man who, in sporting parlance, was willing always "to take a chance" to beat any one he considered his rival. He was taking a desperate chance now. Under the artificial means he had used to increase the speed of his engines, the motor was "turning up" several hundred more revolutions a minute than she had been built for.

Now they shot above the strip of white beach, and, below them the pleasant meadow-lands and patches of verdant woods began to show once more.

All at once, the sign for which Mortlake had been watching so anxiously manifested itself. A tiny curl of smoke ascended from one of the cylinder-heads. A smell of blistering, burning paint was wafted back to the nostrils of Lieut. Bradbury.

"I thought so," he said; "overheating already. Better slow down, Mortlake."

Mortlake glanced back. The Golden Butterfly, much diminished in size now by the distance, still hung doggedly on his heels.

"I'll give her more air," he vouchsafed stubbornly, "that ought to cool her off a bit—that and advanced spark."

He manipulated the necessary levers, but before many minutes it became apparent that, if urged at that rate, the Silver Cobweb would never reach Sandy Beach without a break-down.

"Hadn't you better shut down a bit? That paint's blistering, as if the cylinders were red-hot."

Much as he disliked to interfere with the operation of the aeroplane, the young officer felt that it was necessary that some means should be taken to compel Mortlake to reduce speed. If the engine became so overheated that it stopped in mid-air, they might be caught in a nasty position, where it might be impossible to volplane—or glide—downward, without the aid of the engine.

"It's all right, I tell you," said Mortlake stubbornly. "We'll beat those cubs into Sandy Beach, or——"

Or what, was destined never to be known, for at that instant, with a splutter and a sigh, the overheated engines, almost at a red-heat, stopped short. The propeller ceased to revolve, and the aeroplane began to plunge downward with fearful velocity.

But Mortlake, no matter what his other faults, possessed a cool head. The instant he lost control of the motor, he seized the warping levers, and began manipulating them. At the same time he set the rudder so as to bring the Silver Cobweb to earth in a series of long spirals. The maneuver was that of volplaning, and has been performed successfully by several aviators whose engines have suddenly ceased to work while in mid-air. The young officer watched approvingly. Whatever else Mortlake might be—and Lieut. Bradbury had not taken a violent fancy to him—he was a master of the aerial craft.

Despite the mishap to the engine—caused by his own carelessness—Mortlake managed to bring the Silver Cobweb to a gentle landing in a broad, flat meadow, inhabited by some spotted cows, which fled in undignified panic as the monster, silent now, swooped down like a bolt from the blue.

The instant the Silver Cobweb came to rest Mortlake's restless eyes glanced upward. He was hoping against all common sense that the young Prescotts had not seen his mishap, or at least that they would pass on above him unnoticing. His first glance showed him the Golden Butterfly still steadily plugging along, and a moment later it became apparent that they had seen the sudden descent of the Cobweb, for the aeroplane was seen to dip and glide lower, much as a mousing hawk can be seen to do.

"Hard luck," murmured the young naval officer, as Mortlake, who had clambered out of the machine, stamped and fumed by its side. Inwardly Lieut. Bradbury was thinking how stubborn men invariably meet with some mishap or accident.

"Yes, beastly hard luck," agreed Mortlake readily. "I see a farm-house over there, though, the other side of those trees. I guess I can get a bucket and some water over there. Once I've cooled those cylinders off, we'll be all right."

"How long will that take, do you think?" inquired the officer, pulling out his watch and a time-table.

"Not more than half an hour. It shouldn't take that."

"That means I miss my train. If we don't get into Sandy Beach by eleven o'clock, I can't possibly make it. And there's not another from there for two hours. That would make me late for my appointment at Mineola."

Mortlake's face fell. Here was a bit of hard luck with a vengeance. It might cost him a place in the contests.

"We can make up time, once we get under way," he said tentatively.

"That isn't it. I daren't risk it. I wonder if I can get an automobile or some sort of a conveyance about here."

"Not a chance. I know this neighborhood. It is very sparsely settled."

A sudden whir above them caused them both to look up. It was the Golden Butterfly, swooping and hovering above the disabled Cobweb.

"Had an accident?" shouted down Roy.

"What do you think? You can see we're not flying, can't you?" bellowed Mortlake, his face crimson with anger and mortification.

"Can we do anything to help you?" came from Peggy, ignoring the fellow's insulting tones.

"No!"

"Yes!"

The first monosyllable came from Mortlake. The second from Lieut. Bradbury.

"If you don't mind accepting a passenger, I should be glad of a lift to Sandy Beach. I've got to make a train," explained the young officer.

In five minutes the Golden Butterfly was on the sward beside the crippled Cobweb. Mortlake's face was black as night. He fulminated maledictions on the young aviators who had appeared at—for him—such an inopportune moment.

"Can I help you fix the machine?" asked Roy pleasantly. "There's nothing serious the matter, is there?"

"Not a thing," asserted Mortlake. "It's all the fault of the men who made the carburetor. They did a bungling bit of work, and the cylinders have overheated."

"Can we leave a message for you at your shops, or would you like a lift home with us?" asked Roy, who felt a kind of pity for the angry and stranded man.

"You can't do anything for me except leave me alone," snapped out Mortlake; "you cubs are altogether too inquisitive. You're too nosy."

"But not to the extent of making sketches and notes, Mr. Mortlake?" inquired Peggy sweetly—"cattily," she said it was, afterward.

Mortlake started and paled. Then, without vouchsafing a reply, he strode off in the direction of the farm house to get the water he needed.

"Now, Mr. Bradbury," said Roy, extending a hand.

The young officer leaped nimbly into the chassis, and presently a buzzing whir told that the faithful Golden Butterfly was taking the air once more.

"Score two for us!" thought Peggy to herself.

From a far corner of the pasture, Mortlake watched his young rivals climbing the sky. He shook his fist at them and his heavy face darkened.

CHAPTER XI

THE MARKED BILL

Some two days after the events narrated in our last chapter, Lieut. Bradbury, sitting in the library of the New York Aero Club, on West Fifty-fourth Street, received a telegram from Eugene Mortlake. He was considerably astonished, when on tearing it open, he read as follows:

"Must see you at once. Have positive proof that young Prescott is about to sell out his secrets to foreign government."

"Phew!" whistled the young officer. "This is a serious charge. If it is proved, it will bar Prescott from bidding for the United States government contract. But I can hardly believe it. There must be some mistake. However, it is my duty to investigate. Let's see — three o'clock. I can get a train to Sandy Beach at four. Too bad! Too bad!"

The young officer shook his head. He had come to have a sincere regard for Roy and his pretty sister, as well as admiration for their resourcefulness and pluck.

When it is explained that during the time elapsing between his lucky lift in the Prescott machine and the reception of the note, that Lieut. Bradbury had notified Roy that he would be expected to report at the Brooklyn Navy Yard, his feelings on learning that there was suspicion directed against his young protegé, may be imagined. Mortlake, too, had received a notice that his machines were eligible for a test, so that there would have seemed to be no object for his acting treacherously. Otherwise, the young officer might have been suspicious. What he had seen of Mortlake had not particularly elevated that gentleman in his opinion. But if he had desired to wrong the Prescotts, reasoned the officer, such a resourceful man as he had adjudged Mortlake to be, would have sought a deeper and more subtle way of going about it.

"And I'd have staked my word on that boy's loyalty; aye, and on his sister's too," muttered the officer, as he made ready for his hasty trip to Long Island.

By this it will be seen that Lieut. Bradbury was by no means proof against the rather common failing of inclining to believe the first evil report we hear. It is a phase of human nature that is not combatted as it should be.

In the meantime, Roy and Peggy had sustained a surprise, likewise. The day before that on which Lieut. Bradbury received the disturbing dispatch, an automobile had whizzed up to their gate and stopped. Roy, Peggy and Jess and Jimsy were at a game of tennis, when a rather imperious voice summoned them, from the tonneau of the machine.

They looked up, to see a remarkably pretty young girl, who could scarcely have been more than eighteen years old. Her eyes were black as sloes, and flashed like smoldering fires. A great mass of hair of the same color was piled on the top of her head in grown-up fashion, and her gown, of a magenta hue, which set off her dark beauty to perfection, was cut in the most recent—too recent, in fact—style.

"Can you direct me to Mr. Mortlake's aeroplane factory?" she demanded in an imperious tone. Evidently the flushed, healthy-looking young people, who had been playing tennis so hard, were very despicable in her eyes.

"There it is, down the road there," volunteered Roy. "It's that barn-like place."

The appellation was unfortunate. The girl's eyes flashed angrily.

"My name is Regina Mortlake," she said angrily. "I am Mr. Mortlake's daughter. He is not in the habit of putting up barns, I can assure you."

"I beg your pardon— —" began Roy, quite taken aback by the extraordinary energy with which the reproof to his harmless remark had been given. But the dark-eyed beauty in the automobile had given a quick order to the chauffeur, and the car skimmed on down the road.

Later that day the Silver Cobweb ascended for a flight. It had nothing more the matter with it on the day of the break-down than the heated cylinders, which, as Mortlake had prophesied, soon cooled. But Mortlake himself did not take up the silvery aeroplane on this occasion. A new figure was at the wheel, clad in dainty dark aviation togs and bonnet, with a fluttering, flowing veil of the same color, which streamed out like a flag of defiance.

The new driver was Miss Regina Mortlake.

They learned later that the girl had taken frequent flights in the South, where her father had, for a time, entered into the business of giving aeroplane flights for money at county fairs and the like. His daughter had taken naturally to the sport, and was an accomplished air woman. She knew no fear, and her imperious, ambitious spirit made her a formidable rival even to the foreign flying women who competed at various international aviation meets.

While his daughter spun through the air, Eugene Mortlake sat in his little glass-enclosed office in one corner of the noisy aeroplane plant. Four finished machines were now ready, and he would have felt capable of facing any tests with them had it not been for his uneasy fear of the Prescott aeroplane. But he had evolved a scheme by which he thought he would succeed in putting Peggy and Roy out of the race altogether. It was in the making that afternoon in the little office.

Opposite to Mortlake sat two men whom we have seen before. But in the cheap, but neat suits they now wore, and with their faces clean-shaven of the growth of stubby beard that had formerly covered them, it would have been somewhat difficult to recognize the two ill-favored tramps who had been routed by Peggy in such a plucky manner. But, nevertheless, they were the men.

"You thoroughly understand your instructions now?" questioned Mortlake, as he concluded speaking.

The fellow who had been addressed by his companion as Joey, at the time they encountered Mortlake and Harding on the road to the Galloway farm, nodded.

"We understand, guv'ner," he rasped out in a hoarse voice; "Slim, here, and me don't take long ter catch on, eh, Slim?"

"No dubious manner of doubt about that," responded Slim. "An' although I'm a tramp now, guv'ner, I wasn't allers one. I've held my head as high as the rest of the good folks of the world. I can play the gentleman to perfection. Don't you worry."

This Slim—or to give him his correct name—Frederick Palmer, was, as he declared with such emphasis, a man who had indeed "seen better days," as the phrase is. Now that he was invested in fair-looking clothes, and was graced with a clean collar and a smooth-shaven face, he actually might have passed for a person in fairly well-to-do circumstances. For the part Mortlake wished him to play, he could not have picked out a better man. Utterly unscrupulous, and with the best of his life behind him, "Slim"—as the tramp fraternity knew him—was prepared to do anything that there was money in. His companion possessed no such saving graces of appearance. Short, coarse, and utterly lacking in every element of refinement, Joey Eccles was a typical hobo. But Mortlake's shrewd mind had seen where he could make use of him, too, in the diabolical plan he was concocting, and the details of which he had just finished confiding to his unsavory lieutenants.

"But say, guv'ner," struck in Joey Eccles, his little pig-like eyes agleam with cupidity, "we've got to have a bit more of the brass, you know—a little more money—eh?"

He ended in an insinuating whine, the cringing plea of the professional beggar.

Mortlake made a gesture of impatience.

"I gave you fellows a twenty-dollar-bill a few days ago," he said, "in addition to that, you've been provided with clothes and lodging. What more do you want?"

"We've got to have some more coin, that's flat," announced Slim decidedly; "come on, fork over, guv'ner. You've gone too far into this now to pull out."

Mortlake's florid face went white. As if he heard it for the first time, the words struck home. He had indeed "gone too far," as the tramp sitting opposite to him had said. He was, in fact, completely in the power of these two unscrupulous mendicants. Making a resolve to get rid of them as speedily as possible, he dived into his breast pocket and drew from it a roll of bills that made Slim's and Joey's eyes stick out of their heads.

He peeled off a twenty-dollar-bill, and flung it with no good grace down upon the table.

"There," he said, "that's the last you'll get till the trick is done."

"Thankee, guv'ner; I knowed you'd see sense. A man of your intelligous intellect, and — —"

"That will do," snapped Mortlake. "Do you think I've got nothing to do but talk to you fellows all day? You thoroughly understand, now, to-morrow night on the road to Galloway's farm?"

"Yus, and we've got a nice little deserted farm house all picked out, where we can keep the young rooster on ice," grinned Joey.

"Well, well," shot out Mortlake, "that will be your task. I've nothing to do with that. Do you understand," he rapped the table nervously, "I know nothing about it."

"All right, all right; we're wise," Slim assured him confidently. "Don't you worry. Come on, Joey. Got the money?"

"Have I? Oh, no; I'm goin' ter leave it right here," grinned Joey, enjoying his own irony hugely.

Still chuckling, he arose and shuffled out, followed by the unsavory Slim.

Outside, and on the road to the village, Slim began to be obsessed by doubts.

"Some way, I don't jes' trust that Mortlake," he said. "You're sure that bill is all right, Joey?"

"Sure? Well, you jes' bet I am. Here, look at it yourself. All right, ain't it?"

He drew out the bill and handed it to Slim for his inspection.

"And the best of it is," he chuckled, while Slim inspected the bill carefully, "the best of it is, that I wasn't conformin' to the exact truth when I told Mortlake that we'd spent all the other coin. I've got the best part of it left."

"Good," grunted Slim, turning the twenty-dollar-bill over and examining the reverse side, "that being the case—hullo!"

"What's up?" asked Joey.

For reply Slim handed the bill to Joey, pointing with a grimy first finger at something on the reverse side.

It was an "O," scrawled in dull red ink.

"That would be an easy bill to identify," commented Palmer, uneasily, "wonder if this can be a trap?"

"Well, keep your suspicions to yourself for a while," counseled Joey; "we don't need to break it till we make sure."

CHAPTER XII

WHAT HAPPENED TO ROY

It was the next evening. Mortlake, sitting at his desk, looked up as a quick step sounded outside. The factory was in darkness as the men had gone home. Only a twilight dimness illuminated the little glass sanctum of the inventor and constructor of the Mortlake Aeroplane.

"Come in," said Mortlake, as the next instant a sharp, decisive knock sounded.

Lieut. Bradbury, in a mufti suit of gray, stepped into the office.

"Ah, good evening, lieutenant," said Mortlake, rising clumsily to his feet and offering a chair, "I was beginning to despair of you."

Bradbury, genuinely worried, lost no time in plunging into the object of the interview.

"That message you sent me—what does it mean?" he asked. "I can scarcely believe——"

"Nor could I, at first," said Mortlake, with assumed sorrow. "It cut me pretty deep, I tell you, to think that a boy who was in negotiations with his own government for a valuable implement of warfare, should deal with a foreign government at the same time. In brief, this young traitor is balancing the profits and will sell out to the highest bidder."

"That's strong language, Mortlake," said the young officer, drumming the table with his fingers impatiently. Honorable and upright in all his dealings, the young officer had no liking for the business in hand. Yet it was his duty to see the thing through now, unpleasant as it promised to be.

"Strong language?" echoed Mortlake. "Yes, it is strong language, but not a bit more emphatic than the case warrants. Did you know that for some days past a German spy has been in Sandy Beach?"

"No. Certainly not."

"Well, there has been. He visited this plant with proposals to turn over our aeronautic secrets to his government, but we refused to have anything to do with his scheming."

"Yes, very good. Go on, please." The young officer felt that Mortlake was approaching the climax of his story.

"One of our men," resumed Mortlake, in even tones, in which he cunningly managed to mingle a note of regret, "one of our men took upon himself—loyal fellow—to watch this spy. He reported to me some days ago that the man was in negotiation with young Prescott."

"Good heavens!"

"I know it sounds incredible, but we are dealing with facts. Well, more than this, my zealous workman ascertained that young Prescott is to meet this foreign agent at nine o'clock to-night on a lonely road, and is there to hand over to him the complete plans and specifications of the Prescott aeroplane."

"It's unbelievable, horrible. And in the face of this, do you mean to say that the boy would dare to keep up his apparent negotiations with the United States?"

"That's just the worst part of it, as I understand it," rejoined Mortlake. "The negotiations with this foreigner would, of course, be presumed by young Prescott to be secret. This being so, he would, if successful in the tests, sell his ideas to the United States also, without mentioning the fact that they had already been bought and paid for."

"Monstrous!"

"Just what I said when I heard of it. I could not believe it, in fact. The boy has always seemed to be all that was upright and honest. It just shows how we can be mistaken in a person."

"I cannot credit it yet, Mortlake."

"It was to give you proof positive that I summoned you here. We will take an automobile out to the spot where young Prescott is to meet the foreign agent. Of course, our arrival will be so calculated as to give us time to secrete ourselves before Prescott and the other meet. Are you willing to let your estimate of young Prescott stand or fall by this meeting?"

"I am, yes," replied Lieut. Bradbury, breathing heavily. "The young scoundrel, if he is caught red-handed, I will see if there is not some law that will operate to take care of his case."

Mortlake could hardly conceal a smile. His plan to ruin Roy was working to perfection. In his imagination he saw the Prescott aeroplane eliminated as a naval possibility, and the field clear for the selection of the Mortlake machine. Mentally he was already adding up the millions of profit that would accrue to him.

Lieut. Bradbury left that meeting heavy of heart. Mortlake's story had been so circumstantial, so full of detail, that it hardly left room for doubt. And then, too, he had offered to produce positive proof, to allow the officer to witness the actual transaction.

"Good heavens, isn't there any good in the world?" thought the officer, as the hack in which he had driven out to the Mortlake plant drove him back to the village. Mortlake had agreed to call for him at the little hotel at eight o'clock. The hours till then seemed to have leaden feet to the anxious young officer.

It was shortly before this that Roy, returning from an errand in town in the Prescott automobile, was halted at the roadside by a figure which stepped from the hedge-row, and, holding up a cautioning finger, uttered a sharp:

"Hist!"

Roy, turning, saw a man, seemingly a workingman, from his overalls, at the side of the machine.

"What is it? What do you want?" demanded Roy.

"I have a message for you," said the man, speaking in a slightly foreign accent; "you are in great danger. Your enemies plot it."

"My enemies!" exclaimed Roy.

"Yes, your enemies at the Mortlake factory."

"Let's see," said Roy thoughtfully, "you're one of the workmen at the Mortlake plant, aren't you?"

"I was once," said the man, with a vindictive inflection, "but I am so no longer. Mortlake discharged me."

"Discharged you, eh? Well, what's that got to do with me?"

Roy looked curiously at the man.

"Just this much. I know the meanness that Mortlake plans to do to you. You have bad and wicked enemies at our place."

"Humph! I guess there may be some truth in that," said Roy with a rather grim inflection. "Well, what do you want me to do about it?"

"Just this: I am an honest man. I do not want to see harm come to you or to your sister." This was touching Roy in a tender spot.

"To my sister!" he exclaimed. "Do you mean to say that Mortlake is scoundrel enough to plot against her, too?"

"In this way," explained the man, "he means to destroy your aeroplane, leaving the field clear for his own type to be selected by the navy."

"The — the — the ruffian!" panted Roy, now thoroughly aroused. "Tell me more about this."

"I cannot," rejoined the workman, "but my partner — he was discharged too — he can tell you much, much more. Will you meet him? I can take you to him?"

Roy thought a moment. The man seemed to be wholly honest and in earnest.

"How far from here is the place where your partner is?" he asked.

"Oh, not so very far. We soon get there in your fine machine. Will you go?"

"Well, I—yes, I'll go. Come on, get in."

The man obeyed the invitation with alacrity. Under his directions, Roy swung the car off upon a by-road after they had gone some few hundred yards.

"Not long now," he said, as the vehicle bounced and jounced over the ruts and stones of the little-used thoroughfare.

"This is a funny direction for your partner to live in," said Roy at length. "There are not many dwellings out this way, nothing but a big swamp, as I recollect it."

"My partner, he poor man," was the rejoinder. "He live with cousins out here."

The answer lulled Roy's rousing suspicions.

"It must be all right," he thought. "There can't be any trick in all this. It's quite likely that Mortlake does want to play us a mean trick. I can't forget the look he flashed at me the day we took Lieut. Bradbury away from him in that meadow after we had made our first sea trip. Wow!"

Roy could not forbear smiling at the recollection.

They chugged along in silence for some little distance farther, and then the man beside him laid a detaining hand on Roy's arm.

"Almost there now," he said. "Better slow up."

Roy did so. The brakes ground down with a jarring rasp.

At the same moment a dark figure stepped from behind a tree trunk. The man beside Roy held up a hand.

"This is the young gentleman," he said.

Through the gloom the other figure now approached the automobile.

"Do you mind getting out?" it said. "We can talk better in the house."

"Where is the house? I don't see one," said Roy, his suspicions rousing a little.

"It's just behind that knoll. The path is just ahead," said the newcomer.

Roy got out. He was determined to see the adventure through now. If Mortlake was plotting against him, he wanted to know it.

As he reached the ground, the newcomer extended his hand, as if offering to shake Roy's palm.

Roy put out his hand, which was instantly grasped by the other.

"Your friend tells me that you have something interesting to tell me——" began Roy. "I—here, what are you trying to do? Stop it!"

The other had seized his hand in a clutch of steel, and, before the astonished boy could offer any resistance, had wrenched it over in such a manner that, without exactly knowing what had occurred, Roy found himself sprawling on his back.

The lad was helpless in this lonely place with two men who had now shown themselves in their true and sinister character.

CHAPTER XIII

PLOT AND COUNTERPLOT

The spot was fearfully lonely. Roy realized this to the full. Brave as the lad was, he felt suddenly chilled and creepy. Besides, the utter mystery that enveloped the affair was gruelling to the mind.

"Now be still," pleaded the late guide, as Roy, full of fight, jumped to his feet and flung off the detaining hold which had been laid on him.

"Yep. We don't want to hurt you," chimed in another voice, the voice of the powerful, stockily-built man who had thrown him, "be reasonable and quiet now, and you'll come to no harm. If not— —" he drew a pistol and presented it at the boy's head.

The hint was rough but effectual. Roy saw that it would be mere folly to attempt resistance.

"What's the meaning of this rough behavior?" he asked in a steady voice, mentally resigning himself to the inevitable.

"You just come with us for a little while," said the gruff-voiced one. "Don't worry; we ain't goin' ter harm you. You'll git loose agin after a while. Don't worry about that."

This assurance, though mysterious, was more or less comforting. But Roy resented the utter mystery of the affair.

"But what's it all for?" he protested. "Is Mortlake at the back of it; or — "

"Now, you come along, young feller," said a gruff voice, "don't axe no questions and you won't git told no lies, see?"

Roy saw.

"Well, go ahead, since I'm in your power," he said. "But I warn you it will go hard with you if ever I am able to set justice on your track."

"Hard words break no bones, guv'ner," came from the gruff-voiced man, who was none other than Joey Eccles, disguised with a big beard. The man

73

who had escorted Roy into the trap was, in truth, a former workman at the Mortlake factory, who had been discharged for incompetency. He had applied at the plant to be taken on again, being well-nigh desperate with hunger, and Mortlake had assigned him to the present task, for which, if the truth be told, he had no great liking.

"Where do you want me to go?" was Roy's next question, as neither of his captors had yet made a move.

"We'll show you fast enough, young guv'ner," said Joey through his beard. "Come on, this way."

He caught hold of Roy's arm and began piloting him along a path, or rather cow track, that ran across the meadow. It was now almost dark, and Roy, after they had gone a few steps, was only able to make out the dark outlines of what seemed to be a small hut on the edge of a dense woods lying directly ahead of them.

"I suppose that's our destination," thought the boy. "Well, they have not attempted any violence, and I guess if they had meant me any physical harm they would have attacked me when they first trapped me. But what does all this mean? That's the question."

Nothing more was said as the three, the captors and the prisoner, tramped across the dewy grass. As they drew closer to the building Roy had descried, he saw that it was a dilapidated looking affair. Shutters hung crazily from a single hinge, broken window-panes looked disconsolately out. In the roof was a yawning gap, from which a great owl flapped as they drew closer. Evidently the place had not been occupied as a dwelling for many years.

The door, however, was open, and, with the pistol still menacing him, Roy was marched by his captors into the moldy, smelling place.

Handing his pistol to the other man, gruff-voice—otherwise Joey Eccles—struck a match. Carefully screening it from the draughts which swept through the rickety building, he led the way into a bare room in which was a tumble-down table and two boxes to serve as seats. A pack of greasy cards lay on the table-top, showing that Joey had been passing his time at solitaire.

This fact showed Roy that the plot had been carefully concocted, and that the trap was all ready to be sprung much earlier in the day. Only a brain like Mortlake's, he reasoned, could have thought out such an intricate plan. And yet, what could be Mortlake's object?

"Now, then," announced Joey, when he had lighted the tin kerosene lamp, "I'll show you to your quarters, Master Prescott."

A chill ran through Roy at the words. What could be coming now? With his pistol in his hand, Joey gently urged Roy into a rear room, his companion following with the lamp. Once in the room, Joey stepped forward, and, stooping down, raised a trap door in the centre of the floor. A rank, musty smell rushed up as he opened it.

"Thar's your abode for the next three or four hours," he said with a grin to Roy and pointing downward.

The boy shuddered.

"Not in there?" he said.

"Them's our orders," said Joey shortly. "There's a ladder there now. You can climb down on that. Don't be scared. It's only a cellar, and guaranteed snake-proof. When the time comes, we'll lower the ladder to you again, an' git you out."

Roy looked desperately about him. Unarmed, he knew that he did not stand a chance against his burly captives, but had it not been for the fact that one of them had a pistol, he would have, even then, attempted to make a break for liberty. But as it was — hopeless!

He nodded as Joey pointed downward into the dark, rank hole, and, with an inward prayer, he slowly descended the ladder. The instant his feet touched the ground, Joey, who had been holding the lamp above the trapdoor, ordered his companion to pull up the ladder.

The next moment it was gone, and the trapdoor was slammed to with an ominous crash.

Roy was enveloped in pitchy darkness. Suddenly, through the gloom, he heard a sound. It was the rasp of a padlock being inserted in the door above him. Then came a sharp click, and the boy knew that hope of escape from above had been cut off. If the men kept their promise, they would release him in their own good time, and that was all he had to buoy him up in that black pit.

But Roy, as those who have followed his and Peggy's adventures know, was not the boy to weakly give way to despair before he had exhausted every possible hope, and not even then.

But in the darkness he did bitterly reproach himself for falling into the rascals' trap so blindly.

"Well, of all the prize idiots in the world," he broke forth under his breath in the blackness, "commend me to you, Roy Prescott. If you'd thought it over before you started — looked before you leaped — this would never have happened. Anybody but a chump could have seen that, on the face of it, the whole thing was a scheme to entice you away. Oh, you bonehead! You ninny!"

The boy felt better after this outbreak. He even smiled as he thought how neatly he had walked into the spider's web. Then he shifted his position and prepared to think. But, as he moved his foot struck something. A wallet, it felt like; he reached down, and, by dint of feeling about, managed to get his fingers on it.

The leather was still warm, and Roy realized that it must have been dropped into the cellar from the bearded man's pocket when he leaned over to see if Roy had reached the bottom of the ladder.

"Queer find," thought the boy. "I'll keep it. Maybe there's something in it that may result in bringing those rascals to justice."

He thrust it into his pocket and thought no more of it. His mind was busy on other things just then. If only he had a match! He felt in all his pockets without result, and was about giving up in despair, when, in the lining of his coat, he felt several lucifers. They had slipped through a hole in his pocket.

"Gee whiz! How lucky that Aunt Sally forgot to mend that pocket," thought the boy, eagerly thrusting his fingers through the aperture and drawing out a dozen or more matches.

"These may stand me in good stead, now. But I don't want to waste them. Guess I'll just light one to see what kind of a place I'm in, and then trust to the sense of touch if I see any means of escape."

There was a scratch and a splutter, and the match flared bravely. Its yellow rays illumined a cellar very much like any other cellar. It was walled with stonework, well cemented, and there were two or three small windows at the sides. But these, which at first filled Roy with a flush of hope, proved, on examination, to have been bricked up, and solidly, too.

"Nothing doing there," he muttered, and turned his attention to the rear of the underground place where there was a flight of steps leading up to a horizontal door, which, evidently, opened on the outerworld. But this door was secured on the under side by a rusty padlock of formidable dimensions. Roy tried it. It was solid as the Rock of Gibraltar, as the advertisements say.

"Stuck!" he muttered disappointedly; and yet: "Hold on! What about that pocket tool kit I had when I started out on the auto? Hooray! Those chaps forgot to search me. Thought it was too much trouble, I guess. Now for a sharp file! Good! here's one! Now, then, if the luck holds, I'll be free in not much more than a long jiffy!"

These thoughts shot through Roy's brain, as he selected a file from his fortunate find, and began working away at the hasp of the padlock. Above him he could hear the low grumbling growl of the voices of his guardians. But they came very faintly.

"Lucky thing they are in the front room," thought Roy, as he worked on, "otherwise, they might hear this."

At last the file had cut far enough into the hasp for Roy's strong fingers to be able to bend the metal apart. With a beating heart, he replaced the little tool in its case and pulled the ring of the padlock out of the hasp. Then he gave an upward shove, but very gently. For all he knew, the door he was pushing upward might open in another room. But when it gaped, an inch only, Roy saw the faint radiance of a clouded moon. A gust of fresh, clean air blew in his face, as if welcoming him from his noisome depths. An instant later, with throbbing pulses and flushed cheeks, Roy stood out in the open. Above him light clouds raced across the moon, alternately obscuring and revealing the luminary of the night.

But Roy didn't linger. He crept across the field, keeping close to a tall, dark hedge-row till he reached the automobile. As he had guessed, neither of his captors knew how to run it, and it stood just where he had left it.

"Glory be!" thought the boy, climbing in, "I'm all right, now. I don't know where this road goes to, and it's too narrow to turn round, but I'll keep straight on and I'm bound to land somewhere."

He turned on the gasoline and set the spark. But the engine didn't move.

"Queer," thought Roy.

He got out and walked round to the front and then the rear of the car. There was a strong smell of gasoline there. Stooping down, he found the ground was saturated with the fuel. What had happened was plain enough. The cunning rascals who had captured him had drained the tank of gasoline. The auto was as helpless as if it had not had an engine in it at all.

"Well, this is a fine fix," thought Roy. "However, there's nothing for it now, but to keep on. Those ruffians are cleverer than I gave them credit for."

Stealing softly toward the woods, the boy sped into their dark shadows. Aided by the flickering light of the moon, he made good progress through the gloomy depths. He did not dare to slacken his pace till he had traveled at least half a mile. Then he let his footsteps lag.

"Not much chance of their discovering me now, even if they have awakened to the fact that I have escaped," he said to himself, as he strode on.

Suddenly he emerged on a strip of road that somehow had a familiar look. He was still looking about when a strange thing happened.

There came the sound of rapid footsteps approaching him, and the quick breathing of an almost spent runner. Then came a sound as if somebody was scuffling not far from him and suddenly a voice he knew well rang out:

"Prescott, you young scoundrel, I'll get you yet!"

The voice was that of Lieut. Bradbury.

"Well, how under the sun does Lieut. Bradbury know that I'm here?" marvelled the amazed boy, stopping short.

At the same instant, from the direction in which the naval officer's shout had come, a slender dark figure came racing toward him.

CHAPTER XIV

HOW THEY WORKED OUT

Roy made a desperate clutch at the figure as it raced past, evidently fleeing from an unseen peril. That that peril was Lieut. Bradbury, Roy did not for an instant doubt, as he could hear the officer's shouts in his undoubted voice close at hand.

The boy's hands grasped the unknown's collar, but at the same instant, with an eel-like squirm, the figure dived and twisted. Suddenly it bent down and scooped up a handful of sandy gravel and flung the stuff full in Roy's face. Blinded, the boy staggered back and the other darted off like a deer.

The next instant two heavy hands fell on Roy's shoulders and he felt himself twisted violently about. And then a voice—Lieut. Bradbury's voice—said:

"Now then, you young rascal, I've got you. What does all this mean?"

"That's just what I'd like to know," exclaimed Roy indignantly, brushing the gravel out of his smarting eyes, "I've been made prisoner and —."

The officer's astonished voice interrupted him.

"What! Do you mean to try to lie out of it? Didn't you just hand the plans of the aeroplane over to that representative of a foreign government whom Mr. Mortlake is now chasing?"

Roy looked at the other as if he thought he had gone suddenly mad, as well he might.

"I don't understand you," he gasped. "What is all this—a joke? It's a very poor one if it is."

"I'll give you a chance to explain," said the officer grimly, tightening his hold on Roy's collar, "as things stand at present, I believe you to be as black a young traitor as ever wore shoe leather."

The world swam before Roy's eyes. He sensed, for the first time, an inkling of the diabolical web that had been spun about him.

But it is time that we retraced our footsteps a little and return to events which occurred after the lieutenant had been picked up by appointment in Sandy Beach. In the automobile which called for him were seated Mr. Harding, whom he already knew slightly from meeting him at the aeroplane plant, and Mortlake himself.

"This is a very unfortunate business, hey?" croaked old Harding, as they spun along the road to the place where Mortlake, who was driving, declared Roy had made an appointment to meet the foreign spy.

"It is worse than that, sir. It is deplorable," the officer had said. And he meant it, too. He had hardly been able to eat his dinner for thinking over the extraordinary situation.

But the auto sped rapidly on. Now it had passed the last scattering houses outside the village, and was racing along a lonely country road. Finally, it turned off, and entered a branch thoroughfare which led from the main track.

All this time but little had been said. Each occupant of the machine was busied with his own thoughts, and in the lieutenant's case, at any rate, they were not of the pleasantest.

The road into which they turned was little more than a track, with a high, grass-grown ridge in the centre. It was a lonesome spot, and certainly seemed retired enough to suit any plotters who might wish to transact their business unobserved.

"Bother such sneaky bits of work," thought the young officer to himself, as they rushed onward through the darkness. "I feel like a cheap detective, or somebody equally low and degraded. It's unmanly, and — oh, well! it's in the line of duty, I suppose, or hanged if I would have anything to do with it. Mortlake showed up as more of a gentleman in the matter than I'd have given him credit for. He seems to be genuinely cut up over the whole nasty mess. Well he may be, too."

As described in another chapter, the sky was overcast with hurrying clouds, which, from time to time, allowed a flood of moonlight to filter through. By one of these temporary periods of light, Lieut. Bradbury was able to perceive that they were in a sort of lane with high hedges on each side.

Suddenly Mortlake ran the auto through a gap in the hedge at one side of the road, and drove it in among a clump of alders, where there was no danger of it being seen.

"This is the place," said he, as they came to a standstill.

"And a nice, lonely sort of place, too, hey?" chirped old Harding; "just the place for a traitor to his country to——"

"Hush!" said the young officer seriously. "Let us wait and see if young Prescott completes the case against himself before we condemn him, Mr. Harding."

"Humph!" grunted the old money-bags. "In my opinion, he is condemned already. Never did like that boy, something sneaky about him. Hey, hey, hey?"

The officer's heart was too sick within him to answer. He drew out his watch and looked at it in a fleeting glimpse of moonshine. It was almost the time that Mortlake had declared had been agreed upon for the consummation of the plot.

"At all events, I shall know within a few minutes if this story is to be credited or condemned," thought Lieut. Bradbury.

Old Harding and Mortlake, the latter leading and beckoning to Lieut. Bradbury, slipped cautiously through the alders, and took up a position in the clump at the edge of the road behind a big bowlder, where they could command a good view of the thoroughfare without being seen themselves.

The officer, with a keener sense than ever of doing something dishonorable, joined them.

"Hark!" exclaimed Mortlake presently.

But, although they all strained their ears, they could hear no sound except the cracking of a tree limb, as it rubbed against another branch in the night wind.

"You are sure this was the place?" asked the officer.

"So my man told me," rejoined Mortlake. "You know, I relied absolutely on his word for this thing, all the way through. I, myself, know nothing of it."

He emphasized these last words, as if he wished them to stick in his hearer's memory.

Suddenly, however, a new sound struck into the silence.

It was a heavy footstep, gradually drawing closer. Round the dark corner of the road came a tall form in a long coat and with a slouch hat pulled down well over its eyes.

Lieutenant Bradbury could have groaned. Mortlake nudged him triumphantly.

"Well," he said, "I guess part of it's true, anyhow."

"I'm afraid so," breathed the officer.

"I thought so. Hey, hey, I thought so," chuckled old Harding rustily.

The tall figure came on until it was almost opposite the bushes where the three hidden onlookers were concealed. It looked about in some impatience, tapping one of its feet querulously. Then it fell to pacing up and down.

"Evidently the boy is late," thought the lieutenant. And then a glad guess shot through his mind. "Perhaps the boy has thought better of it."

But even as he felt a great sense of relief at this supposition, there came a low whistle from farther down the road. It was answered by the figure opposite the hidden party, which instantly stopped its pacing to and fro.

"By the great north star, it's true!" gasped the officer, as, from round the bend in the road below where they were stationed, a slight, boyish figure, walking rapidly, came into view. It hesitated an instant, and then, perceiving the tall man, it came on again.

"Have you got der plans?"

The question came in a thick, guttural, foreign tone, from the tall figure.

The boy, who had just appeared, showed every trace of agitation.

"He's struggling with his better nature," thought Lieut. Bradbury. "I'll help him."

He was starting forward with this intention, when Mortlake, prepared for some such move, dragged him back.

"Don't interfere," he whispered, "if the lad is a traitor, as well know it now as at some future time."

Lieut. Bradbury could not but feel that this was true. He sank back once more, watching intently, breathlessly, every move of the drama going on under his eyes.

With a quick gesture, the boy seemed to cast aside his doubts. He muttered something in a low voice, and, as a ray of moonlight filtered through a cloud, Lieut. Bradbury distinctly saw him pass something to the tall man.

"Goot. You haf done vell. Here is der money," said the man, in a low, but distinct tone, that carried plainly to the listeners' ears.

He held out an envelope, which the boy took, with a muttered words of thanks, seemingly.

Lieut. Bradbury could control himself no longer. Flinging Mortlake aside, as if he had been a child, he flashed out of his place of concealment, mad rage boiling over in his veins.

What he had just seen had swept every doubt aside. His whole being was bent on getting hold of the young traitor and trouncing him within an inch of his life. He felt he would be fulfilling a sacred duty in doing so.

But, as he sprang forward, as if impelled by an uncoiled steel spring, the two conspirators caught the alarm. While the officer was still rushing through the bushes, they dashed off, one in one direction, one in the other.

"He's ruined everything," groaned Mortlake.

"No, no; you can save the day yet if you act quickly," cried old man Harding in the same low, intense voice, "shout out that you are after the spy."

"Right!" cried Mortlake, clutching at a straw.

He, too, dashed out of concealment, and took off after the tall man, bellowing loudly:

"You chase the boy, Bradbury. I'll get the spy. Stop you villain! Stop!"

It was at that moment that Roy, just emerging from the woods, heard Lieut. Bradbury's angry challenge:

"Prescott, you young scoundrel, I'll get you yet!"

CHAPTER XV

WHAT MORTLAKE DID

"Look here," cried Roy, indignantly wiggling in the officer's strong grasp, "can't you see that this is all a mistake? If you hadn't grabbed me, I could have caught that impostor."

A great light seemed to break on Lieut. Bradbury.

"Why, bless my soul," he exclaimed, "that's so. I can see it all, now. That chap who got away wore a gray suit, while yours is a blue serge, isn't it?"

"It was, before I was thrown into that cellar," said Roy ruefully.

The moon was shining brightly now, and he saw that, in the semi-darkness, it would have been easy to mistake his blue serge, dust-covered as it was, for one of gray material.

"Tell me exactly what has happened," urged the officer. "I must confess I am in a mental whirl over to-night's happenings."

Roy rapidly sketched the events leading up to his capture and imprisonment, not forgetting to lay the blame on himself for being so gullible as to be led into such a pitfall.

"Not a word more of self-blame, my boy," cried the young officer warmly. "Older persons than you would have stumbled into such an artfully prepared snare, baited as it was with the hope of catching Mortlake in a plot to destroy your aeroplane. But now I'm going to tell you my experiences, and we can see if they dovetail at any point."

But when Lieut. Bradbury concluded his narrative, they were still at sea as to the main instigator of the plot. Of course, the finger of suspicion pointed pretty plainly to Mortlake, but the rascal had covered his tracks so cleverly that neither Roy nor the young officer felt prepared to actually accuse him.

"But I can't see how an ordinary workman would have had either the brains or the motive to direct such an ingenious scheme to discredit me in your eyes," concluded Roy, as they finished discussing this phase of the question.

"Nor I. But hark! Somebody's shouting. It must be Mortlake. Yes, it is. Hull — o — a!"

"Hullo — a!" came back out of the night.

"Come, we will retrace our steps to the auto and meet him there," said the lieutenant.

"I wonder if he'll have the face to brazen it out?" thought Roy, by which it will be seen that his mind was pretty well made up as to the "power behind" the night's work.

"Couldn't come near the fellow," puffed Mortlake, as they came up. "He ran like a deer. But — great Christmas — you've had better luck, I see!"

For an instant, even in the semi-darkness, Roy saw the other's face grow white as ashes.

"He thinks that Lieut. Bradbury has caught my impersonator," was the thought that flashed through the boy's mind.

But the same sudden radiance that had betrayed Mortlake's agitation also showed him that it was the real Roy Prescott he was facing. Instantly he assumed a mask of the greatest apparent astonishment.

"Roy Prescott, I am really amazed that you should be implicated in such a — —"

"Save your breath, Mr. Mortlake," snapped out the lieutenant, and his words came sharp as the crack of a whip; "this is the real Roy Prescott, and he has been the victim of as foul a plot to blacken an honest lad's name as ever came to my knowledge. The young ruffian who impersonated him to-night has escaped."

"Escaped!" exclaimed Mortlake, but to Roy's quick ears, despite the other's attempt to disguise his relief, it stood out boldly.

"Yes, escaped. Partly owing, I confess, to my overzealousness. There has been foul play here somewhere, Mr. Mortlake."

The officer's voice was stern. His eye flashed ominously. Just then old Mr. Harding came puffing up.

"Oh, so you got the boy, hey?" he cackled, but Mortlake shut him off with a quick word.

"No. This is the real Roy Prescott. It seems that a trick has been put up on us all. The lad we mistook for Roy Prescott was some one impersonating him. This lad has been the victim of a vile plot. While we were watching here for his supposed appearance and the revelation of his treachery, some rascals had locked him in a cellar."

The lieutenant's words were hot and angry. He felt that he was facing two clever rascals, whose cunning was too much for his straightforward methods.

"You—you amaze me!" exclaimed old Mr. Harding, looking in the moonlight like some hideous old ghoul. "What game of cross-purposes and crooked answers is this?"

"That remains to be seen. I shall see to it that an investigation is made and the guilty parties punished."

Was it fancy, or did Roy, for a second, see Mortlake quail and whiten?

But if the boy had seen such a thing, the next instant Mortlake was master of himself.

"It seems to me to have been a plot put up by my workmen," he said. "If I find it to be so, I shall discharge every one of them. Poor fellows, in their mistaken loyalty to me, perhaps they thought that they were doing me a good turn by trying to discredit my young friend—I am proud to call him so—my young friend, Prescott."

For the first time, Roy was moved to speak.

"I hardly think that your workmen were responsible, Mr. Mortlake," he said slowly and distinctly.

"You do not? Who, then?"

"I don't know, yet, but I shall, you can depend upon that."

"Really? How very clever we are. Smart as a steel trap, hey?" grated out old Harding, rubbing his hands. "Smart as a steel trap, with teeth that bite and hold, hey, hey, hey?"

"Instead of wasting time here, I propose that we at once go to the house in which Roy was confined, and see if we can catch the rascals implicated in this," said Lieut. Bradbury. "Can you guide us, my boy?"

"I think so, sir. It's not more than half an hour's tramp from here," said Roy. "Let's be off at once, otherwise they may escape us."

"Ridiculous, in my opinion," said Mortlake decisively. "Depend upon it, those ruffians have found out by now how cleverly the boy escaped them, and have decamped. We had much better get back to town and notify the police."

"I beg your pardon, but I differ from your opinion," said the naval officer, looking at the other sharply. "Of course, if you don't want to go——"

"Oh, it isn't that," Mortlake hastened to say. "I'm willing, but Mr. Harding. He is old, and the night air——"

"Mr. Harding can remain with the automobile. There are plenty of wraps in it. Come, Roy. Are you coming, Mr. Mortlake?"

"Yes, oh, yes. Mr. Harding, you will make yourself comfortable till we return."

Having said this, Mortlake came lumbering after the other two, as eagerly as if his whole soul was bent on capturing the two men who had been carrying out his orders.

"I've got a revolver ready for them," he volunteered, as the party plunged through the woods along the little track Roy had followed.

"Take care it doesn't go off prematurely and alarm them," said the officer. "We don't want to let them slip through our fingers."

"Of course not; I'll be very careful," promised Mortlake.

They trudged on in silence. Suddenly Roy halted.

"We're near to the place now," he said.

"Advance cautiously in single file," ordered the lieutenant. "I'll go first."

In Indian file, they crept up on the house. Its outlines could now be seen, and in one window a ruddy glow from the lamp the two abductors of Roy had kindled. Evidently they had not yet discovered his escape.

All at once Mortlake, who was last, stumbled on a root and fell forward; as he did so, his revolver was discharged twice. The shots rang out loudly in the still night.

Instantly the light was extinguished. The next instant two dark figures could be seen racing from the house. Before Lieut. Bradbury could call on them to halt, they vanished in the darkness and a patch of woods to the north.

"What a misfortune!" exclaimed Mortlake contritely, picking himself up.

Lieutenant Bradbury could hardly restrain his anger.

"How on earth did you happen to do that, Mortlake?" he snapped. "Those two shots alarmed those rascals, and now they're gone for good. It's most annoying."

"I appreciate your chagrin, my dear Bradbury," rejoined Mortlake suavely, "but accidents will happen, you know."

"Yes, and sometimes they happen most opportunely," was the sharp reply.

Mortlake said nothing. In silence they approached the house, but nothing save the pack of greasy cards, was found there to indicate the identity of its late occupants.

There was nothing to do but to return to the automobile. They found old Mr. Harding awaiting them eagerly. He showed no emotion on learning that Roy's captors had escaped just as their capture seemed certain.

On the drive back to Sandy Beach, the old banker and Mortlake occupied the front seat, while Roy and Lieut. Bradbury sat in the tonneau. As they skimmed along, Roy drew something from his pocket and showed it to the officer. It was an object that glistened in the wavering moonlight.

"It's a woman's hair comb!" cried the officer in amazement, as he regarded it.

"Hush, not so loud," warned Roy. "I picked it up where I had the struggle with the other Roy Prescott. It may prove a valuable clue."

CHAPTER XVI

MISSING SIDE-COMB

Some days after the strange and exciting events just recorded, Peggy burst like a whirlwind into the little room,—half work-shop, half study,—in which Roy was hard at work developing a problem in equilibrium. It was but a short time now to the day on which they were to report to the navy Board of Aviation at Hampton Roads, and submit their aerial craft to exhaustive tests. Both brother and sister had occupied their time in working like literal Trojans over the Golden Butterfly. But although every nut, bolt and tiniest fairy-like turn-buckle on the craft was in perfect order, Roy was still devoting the last moments to developing the balancing device to which he mainly pinned his hopes of besting the other craft.

From the newspapers they had been made aware that several types, bi-planes, monoplanes and freak designs were to compete, and Roy was not the boy to let lack of preparation stand in the way of success. Detectives and the local police had been set to work on the mysterious plot whose object had been to entrap the boy. But no result had come of their work. Incidentally, it had been found, when the auto which Roy had driven to the deserted house was towed back for repairs, that the tank had been punctured by some sharp instrument.

As for the clue of the brilliant-studded comb, Peggy on examining it, declared it to be one of a pair of side-combs, which only complicated the mystery. Roy had thought of surrendering this clue to the police, but on thinking it over he decided not to. He had an idea in regard to that comb himself, and so had Peggy, but it seemed too wild and preposterous a theory to submit to the intensely practical police of Sandy Beach.

Roy looked up from the paper-littered desk as Peggy flung breathlessly into his sanctum. He knew that only unusual news would have led her to interrupt his work in which she was as keenly interested as he was.

"What is it, Sis?" he asked, "you look as excited as if the Statue of Liberty had paid us a visit and was now doing a song and dance on the front lawn."

"Oh, Roy, do be serious. Listen — who do you suppose has come back to Sandy Beach?"

"Not the least idea. Who?"

"Fanning Harding!"

"Fan Harding! The dickens!"

"Isn't it, and more than that, he is down at the Mortlake plant now. He is going to take up the Cobweb. And who do you think is to be his companion?"

"Give it up."

"Regina Mortlake!"

"Phew!" whistled the boy, "a new conquest for the irresistible Fanning, eh?"

"Don't be stupid," reproved Peggy, severely, "I've been thinking it over and I've just hit on the solution. Fanning, or so I heard, took up aviation when he was in the west. You know he always had a hankering for it."

"Yes, I recollect his fake aeroplane that scared the life out of you," grinned Roy.

"Well," pursued Peggy, not deigning to notice this remark, "I guess they decided that Mr. Mortlake would be a bit er — er — overweight isn't it called? so they sent for old Mr. Harding's son to manage the Cobweb at the tests."

"Jove, that must be it. Makes it rather awkward, though. Somehow I don't much fancy Master Fanning."

"As if we hadn't good reason to despise him. Hark! there goes the Cobweb now!"

A droning buzz was borne to their ears. Running to the window they saw the Mortlake aeroplane whiz by at a fair height. It was going fast and a male figure, tall and slight, was at the wheel. In the stern seat Regina Mortlake's rubicund aviation costume could be made out.

"Fanning has certainly turned out to be a good driver of aeroplanes," commented Roy, as he watched; "see that flaw strike them! There! he brought the Cobweb through it like an old general of the upper regions."

Peggy had to admit that Fanning Harding did seem to be an expert at his work; but she did it regretfully.

"He gives me the creeps," she volunteered.

"There's nothing creepy about his aeroplane work, though," laughed Roy, "I shouldn't have believed he could have picked up so much in such a short time."

But a bigger surprise lay in store for the young Prescotts. That afternoon they had, as visitors, no one less than Fanning Harding and Regina Mortlake. While Peggy and the daughter of the designer of the Mortlake aeroplane chatted in one corner, Fanning placed his arm on Roy's shoulder and drew him out upon the veranda where Miss Prescott sat with her embroidery.

"I know you don't like me, Roy, and you never did," he said insinuatingly, "but I've changed a lot since I was in Sandy Beach before. Let's let bygones be bygones and be friends again. More especially as in a few days we'll be pitted against each other at the naval tests."

"Of course, if you are genuinely sorry for all the harm you tried to do us, I've nothing more to say," said Roy, "I'm willing to be friends, but although I may forgive, it's going to be hard to forget."

"Oh, that will come in time," said Fanning, airily, "I'm a changed fellow since I went west."

But in spite of Fanning's protestations Roy could not help feeling a sensation of mistrust and suspicion toward the youth. There was something unnatural even in this sudden move toward friendship.

"It's ungenerous, ungentlemanly," Roy protested to himself; but somehow the feeling persisted that Fanning was not to be trusted.

"How prettily you do your hair," Peggy was remarking to Regina Mortlake in the meantime.

She looked with genuine admiration at the glossy black waves which the other had drawn back over her ears in the French style.

"Oh, do you like it?" asked Regina eagerly, "I think its hideous. But you know I lost one of my combs and — but let's go and see what the boys are doing," she broke off suddenly, turning crimson and hastening to the porch. Once outside she plunged at once into conversation with the two boys, and Peggy had no opportunity of picking up the dropped stitches of conversation. She caught herself puzzling over it. Why had Regina been so mortified, and apparently alarmed, when she had announced the loss of one of her side-combs? Right there a strange thought came into Peggy's mind. The brilliant-studded comb that Roy had picked up! Could it be that — but no, the idea was too fantastic. In the pages of a book, perhaps, but not in real life. And yet — and yet — Peggy, as she watched the graceful, dark-eyed girl talking with splendid animation, found herself wondering — and wondering.

The next day, just as Peggy and Roy were starting out for a run to the Bancroft place, Fanning Harding and Regina Mortlake came whizzing up to the gate in the latter's big touring car — the one in which she had arrived in Sandy Beach. The machine was the gift of her father. It was a commodious, maroon-colored car, with a roomy tonneau and fore-doors and torpedo body of the latest type.

Beside it the Blue Bird looked somewhat small and insignificant. But Roy and Peggy felt no embarrassment. On the contrary, they were quite certain the Blue Bird was the better car.

"Where are you off to?" asked Fanning in friendly tones, while Regina bowed and smiled very sweetly to Peggy.

"Going to take a spin in the direction of the Bancroft's," said Roy, starting his car.

"What fun," cried Regina Mortlake, "so are we. Let's race."

"I don't believe in racing," rejoined Peggy.

"No, of course it is dangerous," said Fanning, "I guess Roy is a bit timid with that old car, too. Besides it's all in the way you handle a machine;"

Roy flushed angrily.

"I guess this 'old car,' as you call it, could give yours a tussle if it comes down to it," he said sharply.

Peggy tugged his sleeve. She saw where this would lead too. She saw, too, that Fanning was anxious to provoke Roy into a race. Presumably he was anxious to humiliate the boy in Regina Mortlake's eyes.

"Well, do you want to race then?" asked Regina, provokingly, her fine eyes flashing, "there's a bit of road beyond here that's quite broad and one hardly ever meets anything."

Now Roy was averse, as are most boys, to being thought a "'fraid cat," and the almost openly taunting air with which the girl looked at him angered him almost to desperation.

"Very well," he said, "we'll race you when we get to that bit of road."

"Oh, Roy, what are you saying," pleaded Peggy, "it's all a trick to humiliate us. The Blue Bird can't possibly keep up with their car, and — —." But Roy checked her impatiently.

"You don't think I'm going to allow Fanning Harding to scare me out of anything, do you?" he demanded in as near to a rough tone of voice as he had ever used to his sister.

Poor Peggy felt the stinging tears rise. But she said nothing. The next moment the cars began to glide off, running side by side on the broad country road. Faster and faster they went. The speed got into Roy's head. He began to let the Blue Bird out, and then Fanning Harding, for the first time seemingly, realized what a formidable opponent he was placed in contact with.

As they reached the bit of road previously agreed upon as a race course, the banker's son stopped his machine and hailed Roy to do the same.

"Tell you what we'll do to make this interesting," he said, "we'll change machines. Or are you afraid to drive mine?"

"I'll drive it," said Roy recklessly, in spite of Peggy's quavered: "Say no."

"Good. That will give us a fine opportunity to compare the two machines," cried Fanning Harding.

He jumped from the bigger car and handed out his companion. Then, for the fraction of a minute, he bent, monkey wrench in hand, above one of the forward wheels.

"A bolt had worked loose," he explained.

"Come on Peggy," urged Roy, and against her better judgment Peggy, as many another girl has done before her, obeyed the summons, although an intuition warned her that something was not just right.

"Ready?" cried Fanning from the Blue Bird.

"All ready"; hailed back Roy, who found the spark and throttle adjustments of the maroon car perfectly simple.

"Then — go!" almost screamed Regina Mortlake. Peggy was looking at her at the moment, and she was almost certain she saw a look of hatred flash across the girl's countenance. But before she could give the matter any more thought the maroon car shot forward. Close alongside came the Blue Bird.

Motor hood to motor hood they thundered along at a terrific pace. The road shot by on either side like a brown and green blur.

"Faster!" Peggy heard Fanning shout somewhere out of the dust cloud.

Whi-z-z-z-z-z-z! It was wild, exciting—dangerous!

"Roy," gasped Peggy, "if——"

But she got no further. There was a sudden soul-shaking shock. The front of the car seemed to plough into the ground. A rending, splitting noise filled the air.

The car stopped short, and its boy and girl occupants were hurtled, like projectiles, into the storm center of disaster.

CHAPTER XVII

JIMSY'S SUSPICIONS ARE ROUSED

Peggy, after a moment in which the entire world seemed spinning about her crazily, sat up. She had landed in a ditch, and partially against a clump of springy bushes, which had broken the force of her fall. In fact, she presently realized, that by one of those miraculous happenings that no one can explain, she was unhurt.

The automobile, its hood crushed in like so much paper, had skidded into the same ditch in which Peggy lay, and bumped into a small tree which it had snapped clean off. But the obstacle had stopped it.

One wheel lay in the roadway. Evidently it had come off while the machine was at top speed, and caused the crash. But Peggy noted all these things automatically. She was looking about her for Roy.

From a clump of bushes close by there came a low groan of pain. The girl sprang erect instantly, forgetting her own bruises and shaken nerves in this sign that her brother was in pain. In the meantime, Fanning and Regina Mortlake had stopped and turned the Blue Bird. They came back to the scene of the wreck with every expression of concern on their faces.

Roy lay white and still in the midst of the brush into which he had been hurled. There was a great cut across his forehead, and in reply to Peggy's anxious inquiries, the lad, who was conscious, said that he thought that his ankle had been broken. Peggy touched the ankle he indicated, and light as her fingers fell upon it, the boy uttered an anguished moan.

"Oh, gee, Peg!" he cried bravely, screwing up his face in his endeavor not to make an outcry, "that hurts like blazes."

"Poor boy," breathed Peggy tenderly, "I'm so sorry."

"I'm so glad you're not hurt, Sis," said the boy, "I don't matter much. I wish you could stop this bleeding above my eye, though."

Peggy ripped off a flounce of her petticoat and formed it into a bandage.

"Can I help. I'm so sorry."

The voice was Fanning Harding's. He stood behind her with Regina at his side.

"Oh, how dreadful." exclaimed the dark-eyed girl, with a shudder, "my—my poor car."

"And my poor brother," snapped out Peggy, indignantly, "if it hadn't been for your stupid idea of racing this wouldn't have happened. I just knew we'd have an accident."

"It's too bad," repeated Fanning, "but can't I do something?"

"Yes, get me some water. There's a brook a little way down this road. You'll find a tin cup under the rear seat in our machine."

Fanning, perhaps glad to escape Peggy's righteous anger, hastened off on the errand. Regina flounced down on a stone by the roadside and moaned.

"Oh, this is fearful. Why can't we get a doctor? Oh, my poor car. It will never be the same again."

"Nonsense," said Peggy, sharply, "it can easily be repaired. But you don't think I'm worrying about your car now, do you?"

"I don't know, I'm sure," quavered Regina, "I know it's all terrible. Is your brother badly hurt?"

"No. Fortunately he only has this cut in his head and a broken ankle. It might have been far worse."

Regina wandered away. Somehow she felt that Peggy had taken a sudden dislike to her. She sauntered toward the car. Suddenly she stopped and her large eyes grew larger. In the middle of the road, just as they had been hurled from Roy's pocket, lay a side-comb studded with brilliants and an old battered wallet.

"Oh!" cried the girl, with an exclamation that was half a sob, "oh, what good fortune. So he was keeping that as evidence against me, eh? Well, perhaps this accident was providential, after all."

She picked up the comb and then turned her attention to the wallet. Giving a quick glance around to see that she was unobserved the girl plunged her white fingers into the pocket case. They encountered something crisp and crackly. She drew the object out.

"A twenty-dollar bill!" she exclaimed wonderingly, "and nothing else. I wonder if this can have anything to do with — —."

She was turning it over curiously as she spoke. Suddenly a red spot flamed up in her either cheek.

"It's marked with a red round O," she exclaimed, "what a bit of evidence. So Master Roy Prescott, you were planning to unmask me by that side-comb, were you? Well, I shall play the same trick on you with this bill."

Fanning Harding was coming back at that moment with the cup full of water. The girl checked him with an excited gesture.

"Fortune has played into our hands," she cried, "look here!"

"Well, what is it?" asked Fanning, rather testily.

"This bill. Don't you see it's one of the stolen ones. Look at the red circle upon the back."

"Jove! So it is. But, what, how — —"

"Hush! Don't talk so loud. This wallet, which contained it, was jolted out of Roy Prescott's pocket when he was hurled from the machine. The wallet and — and something else. But don't you see what power that gives us?"

"No. I confess I'm stupid, but — —"

"Oh, how dense you boys are," exclaimed Regina, with an impatient stamp of the foot, "don't you see that this bill will come pretty close to proving Roy Prescott a thief, if we want to use it that way? You are a witness that I

101

found it in his wallet which had been jerked out of his pocket. Isn't that enough?"

"Well, men have been sent to prison on less evidence," said Fanning, with a shrug; "but I've got to hurry up with this water or they'll suspect something. I'll talk more with you about this later on. Your father and mine need every bit of fighting material they can get hold of, if we are to win the big prize for the Mortlake aeroplane."

A shadow fell athwart the road as Fanning, an evil smile on his flabby, pale face, hastened down into the depression in which Roy, with Peggy bending above him, still lay. The girl looked swiftly up. A big, red aeroplane was hovering on high. Presently one of its occupants, a girl peered over the edge. The next minute she turned and said something in an excited tone to her companion. The aeroplane began to drop rapidly. In a few seconds it came to earth in the roadway, not a stone's throw from the wrecked auto and its uninjured Blue Bird comrade.

The new arrivals were Jimsy and Jess. They had set out on a sky cruise to the Prescott home, and Jess's bright eyes had espied the confusion in the road beneath them as they flew over. The swift descent had been the result.

Hardly noticing Regina, who regarded them curiously, the young sky sailors hastened toward the spot in which, from on high, they had seen the injured boy lying. A warm wave of gratitude swept over Peggy as she looked up at the sound of footsteps and saw who the newcomers were. In an emergency like the present one she could not wish for two better helpers than the Bancrofts.

Jess and Jimsy had been off on a visit and so had not been made aware of the fact that Fanning had returned to Sandy Beach. Their astonishment on seeing him may be imagined. Jess regarded him with a tinge of disdain, but the frank and open Jimsy grasped the outstretched hand which the son of the Sandy Beach banker extended to him. Evidently Fanning's policy was one of conciliation and he meant to press it to the uttermost.

"Well, this is a nice fix, isn't it?" murmured Roy, smiling pluckily, as the Bancrofts came toward him with pitying looks, "but where in the world did you come from?"

"From yonder sky," grinned Jimsy, trying, not very successfully, to assume an inanely cheerful tone, "not badly hurt, old man, are you?"

"No. Just this wallop over my eye and a twisted ankle. Thought it was broken at first, but I guess it isn't."

"How did it all happen?"

Peggy explained. Jimsy whistled.

"What make of machine is your car, Fanning?" he asked.

"A Dashaway," was the rejoinder.

"The same type as ours," exclaimed young Bancroft. "They are the best and stanchest cars on the market. I can't understand how such an accident could have happened, unless — —," he paused and then went on resolutely, "unless the car had been tampered with."

"What an idea!" shrilled Regina, who had now joined the group, "you don't surely mean to insinuate? Why the damage done to my poor machine will cost a lot to repair, and — —."

"Don't mind if I have a look at it, do you?" asked Jimsy in his most careless manner, "I'm interested, you know. A motor bug is what dad calls me."

"Well I — —," began Fanning.

But Regina interrupted him with strange eagerness.

"Oh, by no means. Look at it all you wish. I only hope you can find some explanation for this regrettable accident."

"I hope so, too," said Jimsy gravely, "but in the meantime let's make Roy comfortable in the Blue Bird. Then, if we can fix your car up, Miss — —."

"Oh, I beg your pardon," struck in Peggy, "Jimsy, this is Miss Mortlake, Fanning you know. Miss Mortlake these are our particular chums, Jess and Jimsy Bancroft."

"Indeed. I have heard a great deal about you," vouchsafed Regina, as Jimsy and Fanning lifted Roy and carried him to the Blue Bird and made him comfortable on the cushions.

"I'll attend to the other car," volunteered Fanning, readily. But Jimsy was not to be put off in this way.

"I'd like to have a look at it before we try to put the wheel back," he said; "it may be a useful bit of experience."

"All right," assented Fanning, rather sullenly, "if you insist; but I think we ought to hurry back at once."

"By all means," quoth the bland Jimsy, "but—hullo, what's this!" He was stooping over the wheels now. "This wheel has been tampered with. The holding cap must have been partially unscrewed. Look here!"

He held up the brass cap which was supposed to keep the wheel on its axle.

"Some of the threads have been filed out of this," he said positively.

"Let's have a look," said Fanning eagerly. He leaned over and scrutinized the part which Jimsy was examining.

"Those threads haven't been filed," he said, "they've worn. Very careless not to have noticed that. It's surprising that it held on so long."

"It might have held for a year if the car was run at average speed," said Jimsy slowly, "but the minute it was raced beyond its normal rate the weak part would have gone."

"What do you mean to imply?" blustered Fanning, though his face was pale and his breath came quickly.

"I don't imply anything," said Jimsy slowly, "but I'd like to know who filed this cap down."

"Pshaw! You are dreaming," scoffed Fanning.

A dull flush overspread Jimsy's ordinarily placid face.

"After a while I'll wake up, maybe," he said, "and then — —." He stopped.

"Well, let's see about getting Roy home," he said, "Peggy, you can drive the Blue Bird and Fanning and Miss Mortlake can sit in the other machine as soon as we get the wheel back. Then Jess and I will go ahead in the Red Dragon Fly and break the news to Miss Prescott."

Shortly thereafter the two autos moved slowly off, while the aeroplane raced above them, going at a far faster speed.

Regina turned to Fanning.

"Do you think that odious boy suspects anything?" she asked.

"I guess he does. But he can't prove a thing, so that's all the good it will do him," scoffed Fanning, "and besides, if they get too gay we've got a marked bill that will make it very unpleasant for a certain young aviator."

CHAPTER XVIII

A BOLT PROM THE BLUE

The broken ankle which both Peggy and Roy had dreaded, turned out to be only a sprain—affecting the same unlucky ankle that had been injured on the desert. This was a big relief, as a broken joint would have kept Roy effectually out of the aeroplane tests, as part of the machinery of theGolden Butterfly was controlled by foot pressure.

A council of war was in progress on the porch of the Prescott home. The participants were the inseparable four. Peggy and Roy, the latter with his injured foot on a stool, and Jess and Jimsy. They had been discussing the case against Mortlake and Fanning Harding. All agreed that things looked as black against them as could be, but—where was the proof? There was not an iota of evidence against them that would hold water an instant before impartial judges.

"It's positively depressing," sighed Jess, "to know that people have done mean things and not be able to get an atom of proof against them."

"Never mind," said Peggy, "all's well that ends well. We start for Hampton to-morrow and once there they won't have a chance to try any more tricks. Luckily all their mean plans and schemes have ended in nothing. Roy will be as good as ever by to-morrow, won't you boy?"

Roy nodded.

"I've got to be," he said, decisively; "those tests have got to bring the Golden Butterfly out on top."

"And they will, too," declared Jess, with a nod of her dark head, "that poky old Harding and his crowd won't have a word to say when they are over."

"Let's hope not. It doesn't do to be too confident, you know," smiled Peggy, throwing an arm round the waist of her enthusiastic friend.

"As the man said when he thought he'd lassoed a horse but found he'd roped his own foot instead;" grinned Jimsy, "but, say, what's all this coming up the road?"

Sure enough, a small crowd of ten or a dozen persons could be seen approaching the Prescott house. They were coming from the direction of the Mortlake plant. In advance, as they drew nearer, could be seen Mortlake himself, with a tall man by his side and Fanning Harding. The men behind seemed to be workmen from the plant.

"Wonder where they can be going to?" queried Jess, idly. For a few moments more they watched the advancing throng, and then Jimsy cried suddenly:

"Why, that's Sheriff Lawley with Mortlake, and there's Si Hardscrabble the constable, right behind them, what can they be after?"

"Clues," laughed Peggy, but the laugh faded on her lips as she exclaimed:

"Why—why, they're coming here!"

"Here!" echoed the others.

"Yes, that's what they are;" confirmed Jimsy, as the procession passed inside the wicket gate and came up the gravelled pathway toward the house.

Sheriff Lawley had on his stiffest professional air and Si Hardscrabble's chest was puffed out like a pouter pidgeon. On it glistened, like a newly scoured pie-plate, the emblem of his authority—an immense nickel star as big as a sunflower.

"Roy Prescott here?" demanded the sheriff in a high, official tone. He had known Roy since he was a boy, but seemed to think it a part of his majestic duties to appear not to know him.

"Miss Prescott—I—that is—er—this is a very unpleasant business—I hope— —."

It was Mortlake stammering. He mopped the sweat from his forehead as the sheriff interrupted him.

"That will do Mr. Mortlake. Leave the discharge of my official duties to me, please."

"That's right, by heck," chorused the constable, approvingly.

"What's the matter, sheriff?" asked Roy, easily. As yet not a glint of the truth of this visit had dawned upon him.

"Why, Roy, it's about that thar robbery at Galloways t'other night," sputtered the sheriff, looking rather embarrassed, "we've come to the conclusion that you know more about it than you told, and— —," he dived into a pocket and drew out an official-looking paper, "an' I got a warrant fer your arrest."

"My arrest!" stammered Roy, "why you must be mad. What on earth do I know about it?"

"Nothin', only you happened to hev' a marked bill in your pocket t'other day," shot out the sheriff, triumphantly. "Fanning Harding step forward. What do you know about this?"

"Only this, that Miss Regina Mortlake after the automobile accident found a wallet belonging to Roy Prescott in the roadway. She opened it and discovered that it contained a marked twenty-dollar bill answering the description of one of the bills stolen from the Galloway farm house. She made me a witness of the find, and in line with my duty as a citizen, I thought it best to expose the thief, and— —."

Fanning stopped and turned pale as a boyish figure sprang toward him with doubled fists. He shrank back, turning a sickly yellow.

"You contemptible sneak!" shouted Jimsy, whose fists it had been that threatened Fanning.

"Sheriff, I claim protection," said the cowardly youth, shrinking behind the official.

"Now, no fisticuffs here," warned the sheriff, "my only duty now is to preserve order and arrest Roy Prescott on a charge of grand larceny."

Peggy turned white and sick. The veranda floor seemed to heave up and down like sea waves under her feet. But in the next few seconds she regained control of herself.

"Why such a charge is absurd," she declared vehemently, "this is simply spite on the part of our rivals in the aeroplane business."

"Don't know nuthin' about that," reiterated the sheriff, stolidly, "the warrant has bin sworn out an' it's my duty ter execute it. Constable, arrest that boy. Ef his foot is too bad hurt to walk, git a rig an' drive him in ter town."

Hardscrabble, flushed and swollen with importance, stepped forward. He was about to place his hand on Roy's shoulder, but the boy checked him.

"No need for that. Peggy, if you'll have them get out the auto, we'll drive into town at once."

Mortlake stepped forward.

"Prescott," he said, "I hope you don't hold this against me. I— —."

"I don't wish to speak to you, sir," shot out Roy, for the first time betraying indignation, "let that be your answer."

"But I— really, I'm sorry to— Bancroft you'll listen— —"

But Jimsy turned his back on the flushed, overfed man whose eyes could not look him in the face.

"In the future please do us the honor not to speak to us," he said, his voice vibrant with anger.

"Why, if I may ask?"

Jimsy flashed round.

"Because, if you don't pay attention to my request I'm afraid I shall be unable to curb my desire to land both my fists in your eyes."

Mortlake drew back and turned away among his workmen. He did not speak again.

Before long the auto came round. In the meantime Peggy had taken upon herself the task of consoling Miss Prescott. Poor Aunt Sallie, she took the news very hardly. It was all Peggy could do to keep her from rushing out upon the porch and denouncing the entire assemblage.

"That Mortlake," she cried, "I'd like to scratch his eyes out."

The proceedings in Sandy Beach before the local magistrate, Ephraim Gray, were brief. Isaac Galloway, the farmer, told of the robbery and of his knowledge that the marked bill was among the money. He followed this up by relating the fact that Roy had been in the house in the afternoon and had seen the safe.

Then came Fanning, and to the girl's astonishment, Regina Mortlake, both of whom swore to finding the marked bill in the wallet in the road.

"Do you deny that this was your wallet?" asked the magistrate, holding up the leather case after he had examined the marked bill.

"I do," declared Roy in a firm voice.

"What! you did not drop it?"

"I dropped it, but it is not mine," was the stout reply.

"Then what was it doing in your possession?"

"Do I have to answer that question, now?"

"It will be better to—yes."

"Well, then, I found it in the cellar of a house to which I was lured by two men whom I am confident were employed by this hound Mortlake."

"Be careful," warned the magistrate, "Mr. Mortlake is a respected member of this community. Your display of ill-will does you no good. As for your story of how you found the wallet you can tell that to a jury later on. My present duty is to hold you in bonds of $2,500 for trial."

A deep breath, like a sigh, went through the courtroom. In the midst of it an active, upright figure stepped forward. It was Lieut. Bradbury, who had arrived in the courtroom just in time to hear the concluding words. But he had already been informed of the facts, for the story was on every tongue in the village.

"I am prepared to offer that bail," he said.

But Peggy had been before him. With her mine shares she had a good bank account and was able to offer cash security. This was accepted almost before the young officer reached the judge's desk. Peggy thanked the lieutenant with a look. She could not trust herself to speak.

"Of course," said the magistrate, "the fact that the defendant is under bonds will prohibit his leaving the state. That is understood."

Mortlake nudged Fanning Harding. This was what they had cunningly calculated on. With Roy safely bottled up in New York state, it would be manifestly impossible for him to take part in the contests at Hampton in Virginia. While they conversed in low, eager tones, Peggy and Lieutenant Bradbury could be seen talking in another corner. Court had been adjourned, but the curious crowd still lingered. Jess and Jimsy stood by Roy, fencing off the inquisitive villagers and would-be sympathizers. The whole thing had taken place so rapidly that they all felt dazed and bewildered. Suddenly the thought of what his detention meant dawned upon Roy.

"We'll be out of the race for the naval contracts," he almost moaned.

It was the first sign he had shown of giving way. But Peggy was at his side in an instant.

"No, we won't, Roy," she exclaimed, her eyes brilliant with excitement, "I've asked Lieutenant Bradbury, and he says it's unusual, but he doesn't see why a woman should be barred from flying in the contests. There's nothing in the rules about it, anyway."

"Oh, Peg—gy!" gasped Jess, "you would — —"

"Do anything within reason to balk that Mortlake crowd in their trickery and deceit," declared Peggy, with flashing eyes.

"And we'll stand by you," announced Jimsy, stepping forward; "we'll go with you to Hampton, and we'll bring home the bacon!"

The inexcusable slang went unreproved. Jimsy's enthusiasm was contagious.

"Thank you, Jimsy," said Peggy, winking to keep back the tears that would come, "we — we — I — that — is — — "

"We'll beat them out yet. The bunch of sneaks, and it's my opinion that Mortlake himself knows all about who robbed that safe!" cried Jimsy, not taking the trouble to sink his voice.

He faced defiantly about and caught Mortlake's eye. It was instantly averted, and catching Fanning by the arm he hastened from the courtroom.

"I wonder what mischief those young cubs are hatching up now?" he said, as the two hastened off, bending their steps toward old Mr. Harding's bank.

"It doesn't make much difference," chuckled Fanning, "we've got that contract nailed down and delivered now."

CHAPTER XIX

THE GATHERING OF THE MAN-BIRDS

The aeroplanes—a dozen in all, that had been selected by various naval "sharps" from all over the widely distributed portions of the country for the weeding out of the best type—were quartered in a broad meadow not far from the town of Hampton. The locality had been chosen as removed from the reach of the ordinary run of curiosity seekers, who had flocked from all parts of the country to be present at the first tests of aeroplanes as actual naval adjuncts.

Sheds had been provided for the accommodation of each type. And above each shed was the name of the aeroplane it housed, printed in small letters. One of the first things that Mortlake and Fanning Harding proceeded to do on their arrival at this "bivouac" was to make a tour of the row of sheds in search of the Prescott machine. But to their joy, apparently, no shed housed it.

There were machines of dozens of other types, monoplanes, bi-planes, machines of the helicopter type, and a few devices based on the parachute principle. But no Prescott. The names the various machines bore were weird: The Sky Pilot, the Cloud Chaser, the Star Bug, the Moon Mounter, theAerial Auto, the Heavenly Harvester, and some titles even more far-fetched graced the sheds, so that it was small wonder that in this maze of high-sounding names a shed at the far end of the row bearing the obscure title of Nameless missed the scrutiny of Mortlake and his aide.

"We've beaten them to a standstill this time," said Mortlake with intense conviction, "I feel that the Motor Hornet has the contest cinched."

The Motor Hornet was the name that had been bestowed on the machine which Roy had poetically dubbed the Silver Cobweb.

The shed of the mysterious Nameless was the only one of the long row that did not buzz with activity all that day, which was one assigned to preparation for the contests of the morrow. All the other aeroplane hives fairly radiated activity. Freakish-looking men hovered about their weird helicopters and lovingly polished brass and tested engines. The reek of gasolene and burning lubricants hung heavily over the field. Reporters darted here and there followed by panting photographers bearing elephantine cameras and bulging boxes of plates, for the metropolitan press was "playing up" the tests which were expected to produce a definite aerial type of machine for the United States Navy.

But even the most inquisitive of the news-getters failed to get anything from within the mysterious realms occupied presumably by the Nameless. Its roller-fitted double doors remained closed, and no sign of activity appeared about it.

This was conceded on all sides to be extraordinary, but all the speculation which was indulged in failed to elucidate the mystery.

"The Nameless is also the Ungetatable," joked one reporter as he and a companion passed by.

But if anyone had been about late that night, long after the aviators who had quarters at the hotels in town had quitted the field, he would have seen three figures—two girls and a boy, steal across the field from an auto which had driven up almost noiselessly, and unfasten the formidable padlocks on the doors of the Nameless's dwelling place.

This done they vanished within the shed for a short time, and presently thereafter a dark and strangely shaped form slowly emerged from the shed. It was the Golden Butterfly, and the trio of young folks were, as you have already guessed, Peggy, Jess and Jimsy. They crawled noiselessly on board, and a few minutes later, with a soft whirring of the propellers, the Butterfly shut down for precaution's sake to half speed, sped almost noiselessly upward.

The night was a calm one. Hardly a leaf was stirring and the stars shone like steel points in a cloudless sky. The aeroplane, after it had attained a few hundred feet, seemed to merge into the dark background of night sky.

Unless one had known of its flight it would have taken a sharp pair of eyes to have discerned it.

"Say, this is glorious. It's like being pirates or—or something," said Jimsy enthusiastically, as soon as they had reached a height where they felt they could talk without difficulty.

"It's great after being penned up all day at that hotel," agreed Peggy, who was at the wheel, "how beautiful the stars are. Poor Roy, I wonder how he is getting along?"

"You know he was doing splendidly when we left, and he has our telegrams by this time," said Jess; "oh, Peggy, I'm so glad that the board of naval aviation said you could fly the Golden Butterfly."

"Oh, weren't they taken aback, though, at the idea?" chuckled Jimsy; "I thought that dignified old officer would fall out of his chair at the idea of a girl daring to run an aeroplane. I'll bet if there'd been anything in the rules about it, Peggy, they'd have barred you."

"I think so, too," laughed Peggy, "but, luckily, there wasn't. As Lieut. Bradbury pointed out, it was a case of an emergency. It isn't as if I'd tried to 'butt in,' as you say, Jimsy."

"Well, I'm sure I don't see why a girl shouldn't run an aeroplane just as well as a boy. You certainly showed that you could, Peggy, when you raced that train back in Nevada."

"In years to come," prophesied Peggy, "I dare say women as aviators will be as common as men. I don't see why not. Ten years ago a woman who ran an automobile would have been laughed at, if not insulted. But now, why lots of women run their own cars and nobody thinks of even turning his head."

"Hear! hear!" cried Jimsy, "I declare I feel like a lone man at a suffragette meeting."

"Then conduct yourself as if you were actually in that dangerous position," laughed Peggy.

The girl's spirits were rising now under the excitement of the night ride. On the advice of Lieut. Bradbury the party from Sandy Beach had kept closely to their rooms at the hotel all that day. It was at the officer's advice, too, that their shed had been labeled the Nameless.

"If Mortlake was, as I begin to think, concerned in these attacks on you," the officer had said, "I think it would be advisable not to appear any more than necessary. Let him think that you are out of the race."

Accordingly, the Butterfly had been transported secretly and placed in her shed at night. The secret had been well guarded and, as we know, neither Mortlake nor Fanning Harding had even an inkling that the Prescott machine was far — very far from being out of the race.

On and on through the night throbbed the Golden Butterfly, making fast time. At last they decided that it was time to return. The object of the trip, to see that all was in running order, had been accomplished. Nothing remained to do now but to wait for the morrow and what it would bring forth. The nature of the tests had been carefully guarded, and not one of the contestants knew anything about what they were to be till the hour came at which they would be announced from the judges' boat.

Suddenly, as they neared the environs of Hampton and the glare of electric lights could be seen on the sky, Jimsy gave a cry and pointed down below. They were flying pretty low, and in a road beneath them they could see an automobile. Its headlights shone brightly but it had stopped. All at once a sharp shout for help winged upward.

"Hullo!" exclaimed Jimsy, "somebody's in trouble down there. Maybe we'd better descend. That is, if you girls aren't scared?"

"Um — well," began Jess, but Peggy interrupted her:

"Jess Bancroft, I'm ashamed of you. It's our duty to help out if we can."

"At least if it gets too hot we can always retreat," muttered Jimsy.

Under the covering of one of the lockers was a revolver. Under Peggy's directions Jimsy found it. The next moment they were descending rapidly. With hardly more noise than an alighting night bird, they dropped into the lane in which the auto was stalled. As they touched ground the sound of harsh voices caught their ears:

"Shell out now, if you don't want to be half-killed!"

"Yes, come on. Hand over your coin, or it'll be the worse for you," chimed in another ruffianly voice.

"Good gracious!" gasped Jess, "it's a hold up!"

But now another voice came through the darkness.

"I suppose you fellows know that you are breaking the law and in danger of imprisonment if you are caught?"

"Now, what is there that's familiar about that voice?" puzzled Peggy, racking her brains.

"Aw, don't preach sermons to us, boss," came one of the gruff voices, "we needs the money and we ain't particular how we gits it, see. Fork over now, or — — "

The sentence was never completed. There was a sudden flash and a sharp report. The man in the automobile had defended himself apparently, for there came the sound of a heavy body falling, and then his voice:

"I hope I haven't hurt you badly; but you brought it on yourself, as your companion can witness."

The next instant, and just as Jimsy sprang forward from the clump of brush at the roadside which had hitherto concealed the aero party — there came a heavy rush of feet toward them. A dark form, running pantingly, appeared.

Jimsy, with a dexterous outward thrust of his foot, tripped the fleeing man, who came down heavily in the center of the road and started howling for mercy.

In the meantime, the occupant of the automobile had climbed down, and detaching one of the lamps, examined the wounded man lying in the road beyond Jimsy's capture. As the rays of his light swung to and fro they hovered for an instant on Peggy's white, strained face leaning forward above Jimsy's prisoner, upon whose neck the redoubtable young Bancroft was now sitting.

"Miss Prescott, by all that's wonderful!" came an amazed voice.

There was no mistaking that bold, straightforward voice now. It was James Bell, the mining magnate and their kind friend.

"Oh, Mr. Bell," cried Peggy, half hysterically, "we're so glad you've come!"

CHAPTER XX

AN UNEXPECTED MEETING

As Mr. Bell spoke, the fellow who had apparently been shot, leaped to his feet and was about to make off, but the Westerner's iron hand seized him by the scruff of the neck, and brought him up "all standing." Simultaneously, Jimsy's captive gave a wrench and a twist and would have escaped but for Peggy.

The girl seized a small nickled wrench out of the Golden Butterfly. In the dark it looked not unlike a pistol.

"You'd b-b-b-better stay w-w-w-where you are," said Peggy, in a voice which, though rather shaky, was still courageous.

The fellow took the hint, and just then Mr. Bell came up with his capture, who had merely been "playing possum." The two men were thoroughly cowed, and were trembling violently.

"Don't be hard on us guv'ner," wailed one of them; "we didn't mean no harm."

"No; it was just a little joke," protested Jimsy's prisoner, who was standing in the rays of the detached auto light, thoroughly subdued.

"It's a joke that's liable to cost you dear," commented Mr. Bell. "Jimsy," he added, for by this time recognition and greetings had passed between the mining magnate and Jess and Jimsy, "Jimsy, have you got a bit of rope handy, my boy?"

Jimsy rummaged in the Golden Butterfly's tool and supply locker and presently unearthed a coil of fine cotton cord of stout texture. This was speedily applied to the hands of the two men, and loose thongs placed about their legs.

While this work was going forward Peggy had been scrutinizing the faces of the two prisoners with a startled look. There was something very familiar about both of them. All at once it flashed across her where she had encountered them before. They were the two men who had held up Jess and herself in the road to the Galloway farm that eventful afternoon on which they had taken refuge from the storm.

She whispered to Jess her suspicions. Her chum instantly confirmed them. Here was news indeed. After the men had been tied and placed in the tonneau of Mr. Bell's car, Peggy called a council of war. In a few words she told Mr. Bell of all that had happened since they had returned to the East, and narrated the part the two prisoners had played in it.

"Good heavens, just to think I've come to the tame and effete east to plunge into the midst of such an exciting mix-up," laughed Mr. Bell, "I was in Roanoke seeing about the shipment of some supplies when I saw, in a newspaper, that the contests for the naval contract were to take place here. I had had no idea from your letters that they were so near at hand. As I had some time to spare, I thought I'd run over to Hampton in my machine and see how you made out."

"And we providentially happened to fly across you!" cried Jimsy. "Truth is stranger than fiction, after all."

"But what are we to do with those two rascals now that we have caught them?" wondered Peggy; "if we take them into Hampton and turn them over to the authorities Mortlake will know of it and may make more trouble. I wonder if they know much about him and his schemes. I recollect now that I've seen them hanging about his aeroplane plant. I couldn't call to mind then where I had seen them before, but I suppose the shock of coming upon them so unexpectedly to-night jogged my memory."

"You say that they were hanging about Mortlake's place?" asked Mr. Bell, in an interested tone.

"Yes, I'm sure of it," repeated Peggy; "I'm certain of it now."

"We'll soon find out," said Mr. Bell in his old determined manner. He approached the car in which the two bound captives were still huddled.

"Now, you fellows," he said in stern voice, "you know better than I do, most likely, what the penalty for attempted highway robbery is in the State of Virginia."

"Oh, guv'ner, don't turn us over to the police," wailed one of the men, none other, in fact, than our old acquaintance, Joey Eccles. His companion, the angular and lanky Slim, remained silent.

"I want you to answer my questions truthfully," snapped out the Westerner, "after that I'll see what I'll do with you. Now then—do you know a man named Mortlake?"

"Y-y-y-yus, guv'ner," stammered the redoubtable Joey.

"Good. You came here with him?"

"Well, what if we did?" growled the hitherto silent Slim. Paying no attention to him Mr. Bell went on, while his young companions pressed eagerly about him.

"What did you come for?"

Joey seemed about to speak but Slim growled something in a low tone to him, and he was silent.

"Come, are you going to answer?" demanded Mr. Bell.

No reply.

"Very well, I'll drive into Hampton and see if the Chief of Police can't get more out of you."

The mining magnate made a step toward the car as if he were about to carry out his threat. This was too much for Joey's composure.

"We came here with Mortlake to do a little job fer him guv'ner," he sputtered out.

"Oh, you did, eh? Well, what was the nature of that employment?"

"To disable one of them flying machines."

"Which one?"

121

"One that belonged to the Prescott kids. Mortlake said he'd make it worth our while—and—no, you can't stop me, Slim—and then when we couldn't find the machine we was to bust up he turned us loose without a cent of the money he promised us. We was broke, and——"

"And so you thought you'd replenish your pockets by holding up some automobilist or traveller, eh? Humph, you're a nice pair."

"You ain't goin' ter give us up guv'ner? I told you the honest truth, guv'ner. Didn't I, Slim?"

"Yep," was the grunted reply; "and now Mister What's-Yer-Name, what are you going ter do with us?"

"I'm going to take you on a trip," was the astonishing reply.

"On a trip, guv'ner," stammered Joey, all his fears lively once more.

"Yes, on a trip."

The younger members of this strange roadside party stepped forward. As they advanced into the glare of the detached headlight, Joey and his companions saw them. Both men turned away and seemed much embarrassed.

"What are you going to do, Mr. Bell?" asked Peggy, eagerly. The mining man's manner had become almost mysterious.

"My dear, little girl," said James Bell, "can you trust me?"

"Why, of course," came in a chorus.

"Well, then, you'll let me work this thing out my own way and I'll guarantee that things will be straightened out for everybody—are you willing to let me do this and ask no questions till the proper time?"

"Yes," came in a positive chant of assent.

"Very well, then. You fly back to your shed. I'll continue into town. You may not see me for some time. But don't worry. I've got this job in hand now and I'll see it through."

"We trust you absolutely," said Peggy, "and you'll trust us?"

"To the last ditch," said the Westerner vehemently, "and now as there's no time to be lost, we'll go our respective ways. By the way, what time does the first test come off?"

"We don't know yet; but some time before noon. It is rumored that it will be an easy one. They'll work up to the difficult flights by degrees," volunteered Jimsy.

"Good. I'd like to have all the time possible as I wish to do what I have to do thoroughly."

With this Mr. Bell adjusted the headlight he had removed and climbed into his car. With a wave and shouted farewell, he was off.

"Gracious, I feel as if I'd been shaken up in one of those kaleidoscopes or whatever you call them," gasped Jess, "it all seems like part of a dream."

"Things certainly have been happening quickly," agreed Peggy, "but I feel more at ease now than for a long time. Mr. Bell has the case in hand, and — —"

"He'll see it through and fix it right," interposed Jimsy, enthusiastically.

As there was nothing to be gained by lingering about the scene of their strange encounter and stranger adventure, the party of youthful aviators clambered back into the Golden Butterfly and once more winged aloft. It was a short dash to their shed and they reached it without incident. Then, with hearts that felt lighter for the brisk, healthy influence of breezy James Bell, they trudged to the small hotel at which they were stopping, in order to avoid being seen by Mortlake and his aides till the last moment.

CHAPTER XXI

THE START OF THE SKY CRUISE

"The first flight is to be to Cape Charles and return, a distance of sixty miles, approximately," announced Jimsy the next morning. He held in his hand a small blue folder which had been issued to all the contestants. It contained the rules and regulations governing the first day's tests.

A hasty breakfast was followed by a quick trip to the grounds in one of the ancient hacks that seem to swarm in Hampton. If the starting field had been a scene of confusion the day before, it was a veritable chaos now. Smoke and the fumes of gasolene hung like a pall above it. Through the bluish cloud could be seen dim figures hurrying with cans of fuel or lubricant, bags of tools and engine parts.

"Reminds me of circus day," commented Jimsy, looking about him; "hullo, there's the Cobweb out already," he exclaimed presently.

Across the field could be seen the silvery wings of the Mortlake aeroplane. Several figures hovered about her, adjusting stays and putting finishing touches to her complicated mechanism.

Presently a hush settled over the scene, and the party of naval officers, detailed to superintend the start and take the times of the competing craft, came through the crowd. They were directing their steps to an unpainted wooden structure at one end of the field. This building was equipped with various instruments for recording time accurately. From it also would presently be given out the wind velocity and any other data of interest to the aviators.

The party in full uniform swung past our three young adventurers. Lieutenant Bradbury was among them. He bowed and was about to pass on when he stopped and fell back.

"Now, don't get nervous, and do your best," he said to Peggy; "I'm sure that we shall all have reason to be proud of the Golden Butterfly before these tests are over."

"I hope so," rejoined Peggy; "we shall do our best, at any rate."

"I know you will, and now if you'll excuse me I must be hurrying on. The board has an immense amount of work to do before ten o'clock, the official starting hour."

The trio, left to themselves, made for the shed which bore the legend "Nameless" above its door. Many curious eyes followed them as they paused before it, and Jimsy inserted a key in the stout padlock. Who could the two pretty girls in natty motor bonnets, with goggles attached, the plain, heavy skirts and dark shirt-waists be? Speculation ran rife. There was a regular stampede of reporters and photographers to the shed of the Nameless. But when they arrived there, to their chagrin, they found that their prospective victims had slipped inside and only the blank doors greeted them.

Among the crowd that hastened to try to solve the mystery of the Nameless was Fanning Harding, whose attention had been attracted by the rush of the crowd. At his side was Regina Mortlake. They arrived just in time to hear somebody say:

"It's two pretty girls and a good-looking boy. They're just kids."

Fanning and Regina exchanged glances. The girl actually turned pale.

"They are here after all," she exclaimed, "and I thought you said they weren't."

"Well, how on earth was I to know that they had hidden their machine under that name. There are so many freak craft here that— —"

"You are more of an idiot than I thought you," said the girl, impatiently; "all our work has gone for nothing."

"No; there is time yet. If only Eccles and that other chap hadn't decamped like that last night, we might have put them to work to-night."

"They decamped—as you call it—because your father wouldn't give them any more money," said Regina with flashing eyes, "that was inexcusable folly. They know too many of our secrets to allow them to wander about unwatched."

"Oh, two tramps like that wouldn't have the sense to make any use of what they know," rejoined Fanning easily, "besides — —"

But Regina Mortlake's mind was busy on another tack.

"Isn't it against the rules for women or girls to drive machines in this contest?" she asked.

"Say!" Fanning's eyes glistened, "I guess it is. Let's find out. If Peggy Prescott is going to drive that machine we may be able to head them off yet."

The two conspirators hastened across the field to the unpainted wooden shack that housed the committee. A crowd surged about it asking questions and demanding impossible things. It was some time before Fanning, elbowing people right and left as he was, could reach the front. He scanned a printed list of the entries for the contest hung on the wall. As he read it he blamed himself bitterly for not looking at it the day before. Near the bottom was the name "Nameless, entrant Miss Margaret Prescott."

Suddenly the disgruntled youth spied Lieut. Bradbury.

"A moment," he cried. As the young officer turned, Fanning, without a word of greeting, bellowed out:

"Ain't it against the rules for a girl to drive an aeroplane in this contest."

"Not that I am aware of," rejoined the officer. He reached over to a stack of pink booklets.

"Here's a book of rules. Read it."

"Hold on," cried Fanning, as the officer moved off, "I want to make a protest I— —"

"Make your protest in writing. No verbal ones will be considered," said the officer briefly.

126

"But see here— —"

"I've no time to talk now, Mr. Harding. Good morning," and the officer passed on.

The crowd began to grin, and soon laughed openly. This enraged Fanning the more. He angrily shoved his way to the outskirts where Regina was awaiting him.

"Well?" she said, lifting her dark eyebrows.

"Well," echoed Fanning in a surly tone, "it's no go."

"No go. What do you mean?"

"I mean that there isn't anything in the rules, apparently, to prevent a woman or a girl driving an aeroplane if she wants to."

"Come and let's see my father," suggested the girl, presently, "he'll want to know about this. It may mean a complete change of our plans."

"You'll have to change 'em to beat the Golden Butterfly," muttered Fanning; "if only those drawings hadn't been lost we'd have had that balancer, and it looks to me as if we might need it before we get to Cape Charles."

"Why?"

"The wind's freshening. Not more than a half dozen of these aeroplanes will venture up. Bother the luck, if it wasn't for the Golden Butterfly, we'd have a clean sweep."

"This is only the first day," counseled Regina; "the points scored to-day will not count for so very much. There's plenty of time."

"Humph," grumbled Fanning, and as this conversation had brought them up to the Silver Cobweb, he broke it off to communicate his intelligence concerning the Prescott aeroplane to Mortlake, who heard it with a lowering brow.

Bang!

A bomb shot upward and exploded, in a cloud of thick yellow smoke, in mid-air.

"The half-hour signal," cried Jimsy; "everything ready?"

"As ready as it ever will be," rejoined Peggy nervously fingering a stay wire.

The navigators of the Nameless were still inside the shed. The doors were still closed. Peggy had decided not to risk having the machine damaged by the crowd by bringing it out before the very last moment. As the bomb sounded Jimsy drew out his watch. He kept it in his hand awaiting the elapse of the preliminary half-hour.

Outside, as Fanning had prophesied, there had been a great and sweeping reduction in the number of aeroplanes that were to start. The puffy wind had scared most of the entrants of the freak types and only five of the more conventional kind of aircraft were on the starting line. The Silver Cobweb was among them.

Fanning was in the driver's seat. As a passenger he carried Regina Mortlake. She looked very stunning in her lurid aviation costume, and her handsome face was as calm as chiseled marble. Her nervousness only displayed itself by a constant tapping of her gauntleted fingers.

Fanning finished oiling the motor and adjusting grease cups and timers, and straightening up, glanced nervously about him. Still no sign of the Nameless.

"I guess they've got scared off by the wind," he grinned to Mortlake, who, with the elder Harding and several machinists, stood by the side of theCobweb.

"I doubt it," rejoined Mortlake; "it would take more than that to alarm those girls. And just to think that all our trouble to out-maneuver them has gone for nothing."

"You did a bad thing when you let Eccles and that other chap get away," commented Fanning; "I don't like their disappearance at all."

"Why?"

"Well, for one thing, they know a good deal that would make it very awkward for us if they fell into the hands of anyone who disliked us. And again— —"

"Pshaw! You are alarming yourself over nothing. They were well paid and they wouldn't dare to make trouble. If they told about us they'd implicate themselves."

"Just the same I don't feel easy. Hullo! there goes the second bomb. That fellow's just going to touch it off, and— —"

At the same instant the doors of the Nameless's shed were flung open. From them emerged the glistening form of the golden-winged Butterfly. Half a dozen men whom Jimsy had hired pushed the aerial craft rapidly across the field to the starting line. So engrossed was the crowd in watching the other machines that they hardly noticed the arrival of the added starter.

But not so Mortlake and his companions. They watched, with jaundiced eyes, the forthcoming of their dreaded rival, and if wishes could have disabled her, the Golden Butterfly would never have flown on that day.

B-o-o-m!

The echoes of the second bomb rang deafeningly.

"They're off!" yelled the crowd, as if there might have been some doubt of it.

Up into the puffy air winged six aeroplanes. It was a glorious sight. From the chassis of the various air craft the airmen waved farewells to the cheering crowd.

Flying, wing and wing, they dashed off toward where the sea lay, a deep blue patch, beyond the shore. Presently they faded into dots and then were blotted out altogether.

"There's a thick haze out there," said one of the officers, as the aeroplanes vanished.

The word ran through the crowd and created a momentary sensation. Then the big throng dismissed the flying aeroplanes from its mind, and wandered about the grounds gazing openmouthed at the freak types, whose inventors were willing enough—too willing—to explain their remarkable points.

It might be a long time before the first of the homing craft would come in sight and what was the use of worrying about them. Only in the wooden structure housing the naval officers was there any concern displayed.

"If it's thick weather," said Lieutenant Bradbury, summing up a discussion, "they're going to have some trouble on their hands out there."

CHAPTER XXII

THE WHITE PERIL

"What's that? No, not that schooner below there—I mean that sort of whitish drift—it looks like cotton—on the horizon?"

Jess leaned forward and addressed Jimsy.

"You've got me guessing," rejoined that slangy young person.

"Ask Peggy."

"No, I don't want to bother her now. She's got her hands full, I fancy."

The Golden Butterfly was swinging steadily onward above a sparkling sea. The slight haze perceptible from the land was not noticeable to the air voyagers. Below them a four-masted schooner was tacking in the light wind. Closer in shore lay several grim looking battleships and cruisers. In their leaden colored "war paint" they looked menacing and bulldoggish.

Far off, a mere speck, could be seen a dim and indistinct object pointing upward from the cape like a finger. They guessed it was the light for which they were aiming. Peggy's last glance at the compass had confirmed this guess.

Jimsy looked about him. About a quarter of a mile off, and slightly ahead was the Cobweb. The silvery aeroplane was rushing through the atmosphere at a great rate. But profiting by Mortlake's experience, Fanning was evidently not speeding the 'plane to its fullest capacity.

On the other side was a large red biplane flying steadily and keeping about level with the Golden Butterfly. Far behind lagged a monoplane. The other contestants had dropped out of the race. They were so manifestly out of it that their drivers did not care to continue.

A glance at the speedometer showed Peggy's two passengers that they were reeling off fifty-five miles an hour. The Cobweb was doing slightly better.

"We should round the light in a few minutes now," said Jimsy scrutinizing his watch anxiously.

"Will they report us?" asked Jess.

"Yes. There is a wireless rigged up there. The minute we round it on our return trip word will be flashed back to the starting point."

Silently they sat counting the minutes roll by. All at once Jimsy noticed that the air had become strangely damp and moist. He looked up. He could not refrain a cry of astonishment as he did so. The Golden Butterfly was enveloped in a damp, steamy sort of smother. The Cobweb had been blotted out and so had the other aeroplanes.

"Fog," he exclaimed. "What a bit of bad luck."

"It's just as bad for the others," Peggy reminded him.

"Have you got your course?" asked Jess anxiously.

"Yes. Almost due east. But in this dense mist it will be hard to come close enough to the lighthouse to be reported without the danger of dashing into it."

"Are you going to try for it?"

"Of course," was the brief reply. Peggy slowed down the engine. The Golden Butterfly now seemed to be gliding silently through lonely billows of white sea fog. It was an uncanny feeling. The occupants of the machine felt a chilling sense of complete isolation.

Thanks to their barograph, however, they could judge their height above the sea.

"Good thing we've got it," commented Jimsy; "otherwise we might have a thrilling encounter with the topmasts of some schooner."

"I only wish we had some instrument to show us where the other aeroplanes are," said Peggy; "it's hard to hear anything in this fog."

"Maybe it will clear off," suggested Jess hopefully.

"Not unless we get some wind," opined Jimsy; "queer how quick that wind dropped and this smother came up."

Nobody even hinted at the deadly danger they were in. But each occupant of the Golden Butterfly knew it full well. Except for the compass, they had no way of guiding their flight, and to turn about would have been to court disaster. There was only one thing for it, to keep on. This Peggy did, grimly compressing her lips.

"Hark!" exclaimed Jimsy suddenly.

Far below them they could hear a mournful sound. It was wafted up to them in fits and starts.

"Ding-dong! Ding-dong!"

"A church bell," cried Jess, "we must be over land, Peggy!"

The other shook her head.

"That's a bell buoy, I guess," she said.

"I wish he'd tell us how to get out of here," joked Jimsy, rather wearily.

"Who?" asked Jess.

"That bell boy."

Never had one of Jimsy's jokes fallen so flat. He mentally resolved not to attempt another one.

Presently he looked at his watch.

"Almost eleven," he said, "we must have passed the light by this time."

"I don't know," said Peggy helplessly; "if only the chart marked that bell buoy — but it doesn't."

She again scrutinized the chart pinned before her on the sloping slab designed for such purposes. But no bell buoy was marked on it as being located anywhere near where they estimated they must be drifting. Drifting, however, is not quite the correct word. An aeroplane cannot drift.

Its life depends upon its motion. The instant it stops or decreases speed beyond a certain point, in that same instant it must fall to the earth.

This fact is what made the position of the young sky cruisers particularly dangerous. Although the gauge showed that they had plenty of gasoline, the supply—even with the use of the auxiliary tanks—would not hold out indefinitely. If the fog did not lift, or they did not land, sooner or later they must face disaster. Worse still, they were—or believed they were, navigating above the sea.

Had the Golden Butterfly been fitted with pontoons like some of the Glen Curtiss machines, this would not have been so alarming. But a descent into the ocean would inevitably mean a speedy death by drowning.

Suddenly voices struck through the smother all about them. They seemed to come from below.

"It's thick as pea soup, captain!"

"Aye, aye; I'll be glad when we're out of it I kin tell yer. This bay's a bad place ter be in er fog."

"A ship," cried Jimsy. "Quick, Peggy," he almost yelled the next instant. "Set your rising levers."

The girl swiftly manipulated the machinery that sent the Golden Butterfly on an upward course.

But it was only just in time that this maneuver was carried out. All of them had a glimpse for an instant of the gilded ball on the main-mast head of the vessel beneath them. For an instant Peggy's watchful eye had been deflected from the height gauge, and she had allowed the Golden Butterfly to drop almost on the top of some coasting vessel's mast.

The danger over, they could not help laughing at the whimsical adventure.

"Just to think how utterly unconscious those fellows were of the fact that three human beings were hovering right above them and listening to every word of their conversation," chuckled Jimsy; "isn't it queer?"

A little while later a steamer's whistle boomed through the fog beneath them, but as the altitude register showed five hundred feet, they did not bother about it.

"At all events we know we're still above the water and not in danger of colliding with any church steeples," said Jess, and she found consolation in the thought.

"Have you any idea at all as to the direction of the light, Peggy?" inquired Jimsy at length.

"I—I really don't know," confessed Peggy, with a gulp; "everything's mixed up. It's so thick I can't tell anything and I'm deathly afraid of running into the lighthouse by mistake."

"Then for goodness sake give it a wide berth," cried Jimsy; "if we keep on cruising about for a while we'll be bound to land somewhere. Anyhow we've got lots of gasoline, that's one comfort."

It was, indeed. In the steady hum of their powerful motor the young aviators found consolation in that lonely ride through the billowing fog-banks. At all events, there was no sign of a falter or skip there.

"If only we could get some wind," sighed Jess.

"Might as well wish for the moon," said Jimsy; "the air is as still as it used to be at noon out on the desert."

"What a contrast between the Big Alkali and this!" cried Jess, half hysterically. The strain of the white drifting fog was beginning to tell upon her.

Jimsy looked at her sharply.

"Look here, Sis," he began and was going on when a sharp cry from Peggy arrested him. At the same instant the Golden Butterfly swerved sharply, swinging over on her beam-ends almost.

Right in front of them, for one dreadful instant, there loomed the outlines of another aeroplane. The next instant it was gone. But the picture of the deadly peril, its outlines exaggerated by the mist, was photographed in the minds of every one of them.

"We must land somewhere, soon," said Peggy, in rather a faint voice; "I don't think I could stand many shocks like that. Another inch, and — —."

She did not complete the sentence. Her two listeners did not require her to. It did not take a vivid imagination to have pictured the result of that "other inch."

CHAPTER XXIII

OUT OF THE CLOUDS

Ten minutes or so later, a puff of wind blew the folds of fog apart for a brief instant. Beneath them Peggy could see a sandy beach and some scrubby-looking brush. Like a flash she took advantage of the momentarily revealed opportunity. The Golden Butterfly, under her guidance, sank swiftly, grounding a few seconds later into a bed of soft sand. It was like lighting on a pillow of down, so gently had the glide to earth been made.

Shutting off the engine, Peggy took hold of Jimsy's outstretched arm and, followed by Jess, she jumped lightly out upon the sand. The roar of the surf, as the big swells rolled upon the beach was in their ears. A wholesome, stinging tang of salt in their nostrils.

"I wonder where on earth we've landed," said Jimsy, looking about him; "perhaps this is some enchanted land and we are to face new perils — dragons or something."

"Well, gallant knight," laughed Jess, in the highest spirits to be back on the firm ground again — even if it was only shifting sand — "we trust to you."

"And by my troth," exclaimed the mercurial Jimsy, "ye shall not be disappointed in me fair damsels. Hullo! an adventure already. Hark!"

Through the smother a dull sound was borne to their ears. A sound that came in muffled but rhythmic thumps. At intervals it paused, but then was resumed again.

"Somebody chopping wood!" exclaimed Peggy, recognizing the sound.

"That's just what it is, if I ever wielded an axe in my life," agreed Jimsy; "now logic tells us that an axe can't work itself. Therefore somebody must be using it. Where there is human life there is — or ought to be — food. How about it girls, are you hungry?"

"Hungry! I could eat anything," declared Jess.

"I'm almost as bad," laughed Peggy.

"Well," said Jimsy, "as there is no sign of the fog lifting yet awhile, what's the matter with our starting out to find the wood-chopper and seeing if he has anything to eat?"

"Jimsy, you're a genius," cried Jess.

"That's what all my friends tell me," rejoined the modest youth.

They set off over rough sand dunes, overgrown with coarse grass, in the direction of the sounds of the axe. The sand was loose and their feet sank ankle deep in it, but they plodded along pluckily.

All at once, just as if a curtain had been drawn, the outlines of a rough shanty appeared in front of them. It was a tumble-down sort of a place, seemingly made of driftwood and old sacks and bits of canvas. From a rusty iron stove-pipe on top, a feeble column of blue smoke was ascending.

The noise of chopping had ceased on their approach and as they stood hesitating a strange figure suddenly appeared round the corner of the wretched rookery of a place. The man, who stood facing them, a startled look in his light blue eyes, was apparently about middle age. He wore a full beard of a golden brown color and was barefooted and hatless. His clothes consisted of a tattered shirt and a pair of coarse canvas trousers.

"Well, shiver my toplights!" he cried as his eyes fell on the trio, "whar under ther sun did you come from? Drop from ther clouds?"

"That's just what we did," said the debonnaire Jimsy, as the girls drew back rather affrighted at the weird looking figure and his queer, wild way of talking.

"What's that? Don't try to fool with me young feller. I ain't as crazy as I reckon I looks."

There was a certain dignity about the man when he spoke, that, despite his ragged clothing and miserable habitation, was impressive.

"No, it's really so," Jimsy hastened to assure him, "we—we came in an aeroplane, you know."

"Well, now," said the man scratching his head, "I reckon that's the first of them contrivances to reach Lost Brig Island."

"Lost Brig Island," echoed Jess in an alarmed tone; "is this an island?"

"If the geography books still define an island as a body of land surrounded by water, it is," rejoined the man, with a smile.

"Are we far from Cape Charles?" asked Peggy, eagerly.

"Why, no. Not more than six miles to the north. But what under ther sun air you young folks in your fine clothes a-doin' out here?"

Peggy hastily explained, and the man said that he had seen some reference to the coming contests in a stray paper the light-keepers had given him the last time he passed the lighthouse in a small boat he kept.

"Is the island inhabited?" inquired Jimsy; "we'd like to get something to eat. If there's a hotel or — —."

The man of the island burst into a laugh. Not a rough guffaw, but a laugh of genuine amusement.

"I guess I'm the only hotel keeper on the island," he said, "and my guests is sea gulls and once in a while a turtle. But if you don't mind eating some fish and potatoes, you're welcome to what I have."

"I'm sure that's awfully good of you," said Peggy, warmly, "and we love fish."

"Well, come on in and sit down. This fog won't last forever. I was chopping wood to get dinner when I heard you coming over the sands. I don't often have visitors so you'll have to rough it."

So saying, the strange, lone island dweller led them into his hut. It was rough inside but scrupulously clean. Some attempts had been made to beautify it by hanging up on the walls shells and curiosities of the beach. Here and there, too, were panels of rare woods, which the island-dweller explained had come from the cabins of wrecked ships. A big cat, his only companion, lay beside the fire and blinked at the visitors, as if they were an everyday occurrence.

Chairs, fashioned out of barrels and boxes, stood about, some of them cushioned after a fashion, with sacking stuffed with dried sea weed.

"Sit down," said their host hospitably, "ain't much to boast of in the way of furniture, but it's the best I can do. Can't expect to find a Waldorf Hotel on Lost Brig Island."

"You have been in New York, then?" exclaimed Peggy, struck by the reference.

The man's face underwent a transformation.

"Once, many years ago," he said, "but I never like to talk about it."

"Why not?" blundered the tactless Jimsy.

"Because a wrong—a very great wrong—was done to me there," said the man slowly.

Without another word he rose and left the hut. None of the visitors dared to speak to him, so black had his face grown at the recollections called up by Peggy's unlucky remark.

After an absence of some moments he came back. He carried a string of cleaned fish in one hand and a tin measure of potatoes in the other. In the interval that had elapsed he seemed to have recovered his equanimity.

"Well, here's dinner," he announced in a cheery voice, "it ain't much to boast of, but hunger's the best sauce."

Sitting on an upturned box he started to peel potatoes, and presently put them on the fire in a rough iron pot. When they were almost done, a fact which he ascertained by prodding them with a clean sliver of wood, he set the fish in a frying pan or "spider," and the appetizing aroma of the meal presently filled the lowly hut.

On a table formed of big planks, once the hull of some wrecked schooner, laid on rough trestles, they ate, what Peggy afterward declared, was one of the most enjoyable dinners of her life. Their host had at one time of his life been a sailor it would seem. At any rate, he had a fund of anecdote of the sea and its perils that held them enthralled.

Every now and again, through the open door, Peggy cast a glance outside. But the fog still hung thick. Suddenly, in the midst of their meal, footsteps sounded and voices came to their ears.

"Hullo, more visitors!" exclaimed the man of the island starting to his feet, "this is a day of events with a vengeance. Who can be coming now?"

The footsteps had drawn close now and a voice could be heard saying:

"What a rickety, tumble-down old place. I wonder what kind of savage lives here."

"Fanning Harding!" gasped Peggy, as another voice struck in. A voice she instantly knew as Regina Mortlake's.

"Oh, what a dreadful place. Why won't this miserable fog lift. I'll be dead before we get back to the hotel."

The man of the island had hastened hospitably out to welcome the newcomers.

Peggy, Jess and Jimsy exchanged glances. The prospect of spending the afternoon marooned on an island with Fanning Harding and Regina Mortlake, was not alluring. But there was no escape. The next minute the man of the island ushered in his two new guests.

"What, you here?" said Fanning in an ungracious tone, while Regina Mortlake, more skilled at disguising her feelings, exclaimed:

"Oh, how perfectly wonderful that we should both have landed on the same island."

"It wasn't from choice," grumbled Fanning in a perfectly audible tone.

Jimsy flushed a dark, dangerous flush.

"Jess, tell me not to punch that chap," he muttered to his sister.

"I certainly do tell you not to," whispered Jess emphatically.

The man of the island looked on wonderingly.

"Did you come in an aeroplane, too?" he asked Fanning in the manner of a man prepared to hear any marvels.

"Yes. We had the race won, too. But this fog has delayed us. What can you give us to eat. I can pay for it," said Fanning in a loud, rude tone.

"I don't take pay," said the hut-dweller in a quiet tone that ought to have caused Fanning to redden with shame, "but if you are hungry I can cook some more fish. There are plenty of potatoes left."

"They'll be very nice, I'm sure," Regina had the grace to say. But Fanning mumbled something about "pauper's food."

But nevertheless he ate as heartily as Jimsy himself, when the food was put on the rough table. It was hard work trying to be pleasant to the two young people who had so unexpectedly come into their midst, and the conversation languished and went on by fits and starts.

"Hullo, the fog's lifting," cried Fanning suddenly; "I'm off. Come on Regina."

The girl rose, and as she did so the trio from the Prescott machine noticed the island dweller's eyes fixed on her in a curious way.

"Pardon me," he said, "but is your name Regina?"

The girl looked at him in a half-startled way, while Peggy, as she said afterward, felt as if she was watching a drama.

"Yes," she said; "why?"

"Because," said the island dweller slowly, "because I once knew someone called Regina who was very dear to me."

"Come on," called Fanning from outside, "we've got to win this race back."

The girl lingered hesitatingly an instant and the next moment was gone.

"The fog is lifting," said Peggy, "we must be going, too. Come along Jess. Come on, Jimsy, we don't want to let the Mortlake craft beat us at the eleventh hour."

"What name was that you just mentioned?" asked the man of the island, quickly. He was bending forward eagerly, as if to catch the answer.

"Do you mean Mortlake?"

"Yes, that's the name. What of him? Do you know him?"

The man's eyes gleamed brightly. He seemed to be much excited. Peggy answered him calmly, although she felt as if some sort of a life tragedy was working out to swift conclusion.

"Of course, Mr. Eugene Mortlake is the man who is manufacturing the Mortlake aeroplane. He is our chief rival. That's the reason we must hurry off."

"Why, did they?" the man nodded his head in the direction in which Fanning and Regina had vanished, "did they come in a Mortlake aeroplane?"

"Yes," said Peggy, "didn't you know? That girl is Mr. Mortlake's daughter, Regina Mortlake."

The man gave a terrible cry and reeled backward. Jimsy stepped forward quickly and caught him. For an instant they thought their host was going to swoon. But he quickly recovered.

"Good heavens," he cried, "Eugene Mortlake is here. Close at hand?"

"He is in Hampton — why?"

"I must see him as soon as possible. No, I can explain nothing now. But I must see him."

The man's manner showed that he was terribly in earnest. He seemed almost carried away by excitement. Outside came suddenly a whirring sound.

"Fanning is starting his engine," exclaimed Jimsy; "we must hurry."

"Will you do something for me — will you aid a miserable outcast to right a great wrong?" pleaded the ragged man who faced them.

"What can we do for you?" asked Jimsy.

"Take me back to Hampton in your aeroplane. I must see Mortlake at once. It is imperative I tell you. See, I am not poor, although I appear so."

In two strides the man had crossed the room and lifting a board in the floor he drew forth bag after bag. The seams of some of them were rotten. Under the sudden strain they broke and streams of gold coin trickled out upon the floor.

"Years ago when I was first an exile here," said the man, "a Spanish ship came ashore one stormy night. Not a soul of her crew was saved. I found this money in the wreck. I will give you half of it if you will take me to Hampton with you. The other half I must keep till — till I learn from Mortlake's lips the secret he holds."

"Put your money back," said Jimsy quietly after a telegraphic exchange of looks with Peggy, "we'll take you to Hampton; but hurry!"

Fifteen minutes later a golden-hued aeroplane flashed past the Cape Charles light. The announcer posted there, instantly sent in a wireless flash to Hampton.

"Number Six has just passed. Two minutes behind Number Five (The Silver Cobweb), four persons on board."

Mortlake was among the crowd that read the bulletin which was instantly posted upon the field outside Hampton.

"I wonder who the fourth can be?" he thought, little guessing that through the air fate was winging its way toward him.

144

"Anyway," he added to himself the next instant, "the Mortlake is leading. Now if only — —"

But what was that roar, at first a sullen boom, gradually deepening into the excited skirling cheers of a vast throng.

Mortlake looked round, startled. Out of the distance two tiny dots, momentarily growing larger, like homing birds, had come into view. Hark! What was that the crowd were shouting? Those with field glasses threw the cry out first, and then came a mighty roar, as it was caught up by hundreds of throats.

"The Nameless! The Nameless wins!"

Mortlake paled, and caught at a post erected to hold up a telephone line. He gazed at the oncoming aeroplanes. There were three of them now, but one was far behind, laboring slowly. But the first was unquestionably the Golden Butterfly. He could catch the yellow glint of her wings. And that second craft — its silvery sheen betrayed it — was the Mortlake Cobweb, as Roy had called it.

"Come on! Come on!" shouted Mortlake, uselessly as he knew, "what's the matter with you?"

But alas, the Cobweb didn't "come on." Some three or four minutes after the Golden Butterfly had alighted and been swallowed up in a surging, yelling throng of enthusiasm-crazed aero fans, the Cobweb fluttered wearily to the ground, unnoticed almost amid the excitement over the Golden Butterfly's feat.

Mortlake raged, old Mr. Harding almost wept, and Fanning sulkily explained that it wasn't his fault, the cylinders having overheated again. But not all of this could wipe out those figures that had just been put up on the board, which proclaimed a victory for the Prescott aeroplane by a margin of three and twenty-one hundredths minutes!

CHAPTER XXIV

FRIENDS AND FOES—CONCLUSION

The winning of the "Sky Cruise," as the newspapers had dubbed it, was the talk of Hampton that night. Not a small part of the zest with which it was discussed was caused by the fact that a young girl had driven the machine through its daring dash. The wires from New York, Baltimore, Philadelphia, Boston and Richmond were kept hot with instructions from editors to their representatives demanding interviews with the Girl Aviators. But to the chagrin of the newspaper representatives, after seeing their machine housed, the party had vanished.

This, on investigation, was not as mysterious as it had at first appeared. There was a small door in the back of the Nameless's shed, and at this door there had been waiting, for some moments before the conclusion of the race, a big automobile. In it were seated a bronzed man, with broad shoulders, and an alert, wideawake expression, and a boy, whose foot was propped up on an extemporized contrivance affixed to the seat.

While the crowd had hovered about the front of the shed, awaiting the reappearance of the girl aviator, whose feat had caused such a furore, this boy had limped from the machine, assisted by his stalwart companion, and had entered the shed by the rear door. It would have astonished the crowd, and delighted the reporters in search of a story, if they could have seen Peggy rush at the youth, and with a wild cry of:

"Roy! You darling!" throw her arms about his neck.

Mr. Bell, for he was the stalwart personage, stood aside with a look of warm satisfaction, as Peggy's turn over, Jess and Jimsy came forward. What a joyous reunion that was, I will leave you to imagine. Then came Mr. Bell's story of his telegram to Sandy Beach to the judge, who was a friend of his. The message had announced that he had obtained complete confessions from both Joey Eccles and the unsavory Slim. Roy's release from bail and suspicion at once followed.

Eccles had owned up to his part in the mischief that had been wrought against the young Prescotts. Frankly, and without reserve, he had sworn to a statement before a local attorney, in which he admitted losing the bill with the mark upon it, on the night he had aided in decoying Roy to the old house. His assistant had been a cast off workman of the Mortlake plant, of whose whereabouts Joey said he was now ignorant.

Then had come Slim's turn. Sullenly, but with the alternative of prison staring him in the face, he had admitted to impersonating the foreign spy. The part of Roy on that eventful night had been played by:

"Guess whom?" said Mr. Bell, looking round.

They all shook their heads.

"I'll tell you about that part of it later," said Mr. Bell. "There are still one or two things to be cleared up in that connection. But," he continued, "Palmer confessed that it was Mortlake who robbed the farm-house safe, the object being, of course, not so much the money, as a chance to put Roy out of the race contest. It has been a record of vile plotting all the way through," said the Westerner warmly, "but the toils are closing in about Mortlake & Co. Of course, my first step was to take the fellows before an attorney—luckily I knew one in Hampton, and he, as it happened, was a friend of the Sandy Beach judge. We had to move quickly, but, thanks to the telegraph wire and fast trains, I got Roy released from bail and suspicion, and here in time to greet you."

They could only look their gratitude. Just as the strain was becoming almost too taut, Mr. Bell, who had noticed it, broke the tension.

"Let's sneak out of the back door," he said, "and all go to some quiet place to dine. Hullo, who's this?" he exclaimed, as the tattered figure of the man of the island appeared.

"I am what is left of Budd Pierce, Jim Bell," said the man, in his queer, tired tones.

"Budd Pierce!" exclaimed the mining man, falling back a step. "No—but, yes, now I look again—it is. But, man, what has happened to you? What are you doing here?"

"It's a long story," said the ragged man, while the younger members of the party looked on in astonishment, "but I can tell you that Gene Mortlake has reached the end of his tether. I've heard all you said about him, and my interest in him you know already."

"I know that you were swindled out of your fortune by some man years ago, and then disappeared," said Mr. Bell. "But I had forgotten the name of the rascal."

"It was Eugene Mortlake," said the man of the island slowly. "After I knew I was ruined, I fled down here, where I was raised, and became a recluse on that island. It was cowardly of me, I know, but from now on I am going to lead a different life."

"You have found yourself!" cried James Bell, gleefully clasping the other's thin, worn hand.

"I have found something dearer to me," was the quiet reply; "but come, let us be going. I have much that is strange to tell you."

With wondering looks, the young aviators—Roy leaning on Peggy's devoted arm—followed James Bell and the man from Lost Brig Island out of the aeroplane shed.

In his suite of rooms at the Hotel Hampton, the best hotel in the place, Eugene Mortlake sat opposite old Mr. Harding. His brow was furrowed, and little wrinkles that had not been there earlier in the day, appeared at the corners of his eyes. Old Mr. Harding seemed to be trying to cheer him up. In another corner of the room, sullen and depressed, Fanning Harding was standing puffing a cigarette and filling the atmosphere with its reeking fumes.

"All is not lost yet, Mortlake, hey, hey, hey?" said the old man, laying a skinny, claw-like hand on the other's arm. "Why, to-night we'll put into execution a plan that will permanently put these young Prescotts out of it. Fanning knows what I mean. Hey?"

He glanced up at his ill-favored son.

"I know fast enough," said that young hopeful, "but it's a risky matter. Why don't you get somebody else to do it?"

"Pshaw! It's only filing off a padlock and then smashing a few of the motor parts," said the old man, in as calm a tone as if he were proposing a constitutional walk, "that's soon done, hey?"

A sharp knock at the door interrupted any reply Fanning might have been about to make.

"Come in," snarled Mortlake. "It's the mail, I suppose," he said, turning to old Mr. Harding, but, to his surprise and consternation, the opened door revealed Roy Prescott. Close behind him came Mr. Bell and Peggy, with Jimsy and Jess bringing up the rear.

"To what am I indebted for the pleasure of this visit?" asked Mortlake, glowering at the newcomers, as they filed in, and Mr. Bell closed the door behind them. "Why didn't you send up your cards, and I'd have torn them up and thrown them out of the window."

"Just what I thought you'd do, so we came up ourselves," said Mr. Bell cheerily. "Now, look here, Mortlake—no, sit down. I've come up here to right a wrong. You've tried to do all in your power to injure these young people, whose only fault is that they have built a better aeroplane than you have. It's their turn now, and you've got to grin and bear it."

Mortlake's jaw dropped. His old bullying manner was gone now. Old Man Harding cackled inanely, but said nothing. Only his long, lean fingers drummed on the table. Fanning turned a pasty yellow. He had some idea of what was to come. His eyes fell to the floor, as if seeking some loophole of escape there.

"Well," growled Mortlake, "what have you got to say to me?"

149

"Not much," snapped the mining man, "but I wish to read you something."

He drew from his pocket a paper.

"This is the confession of Joey Eccles," he said quietly. "I've another by Frederick Palmer."

Mortlake leaped up and sprang toward the Westerner, but Mr. Bell held up his hand.

"Don't try to destroy them," he said. "They are only copies. The originals are by this time in the hands of the authorities at Sandy Beach."

Mortlake sank back with staring eyes and white cheeks.

"What do you want me to do?" he gasped.

"Listen to these confessions and then sign your name to them, signifying your belief that they are true documents."

"And if not?"

"Well, if not," said Mr. Bell, measuring his words, "do you recollect that wild-cat gold mine scheme you were interested in more years ago than you'll care to remember?"

Mortlake seemed to shrivel. But he flared up in a last blaze of defiance.

"You can't scare me by rattling old bones," he said, "What do you know about it?"

For reply, Mr. Bell stepped to the door.

"Mr. Budd," he called softly, and in response the man of Lost Brig Island, but now dressed and barbered into civilization appeared.

"Pierce Budd!" gasped Mortlake.

"Yes, Pierce Budd, whom you ruined," said Mr. Bell. "But for my persuasions, he would have sought to wipe out his wrongs in personal violence. But you needn't fear him now," as Mortlake looked round with hunted eyes; "that is, if you sign."

"I'll sign," gasped out the trapped man. He reached for an inkstand. "Give them to me."

"I'll read them first," said the mining man, and then, in slow, measured tones, he read out the contents of the convicting documents. As he concluded, Mortlake seemed about to collapse. But he took the papers with a trembling hand, and wrote:

"All this is true. — Eugene Mortlake."

"Good," said Mr. Bell. "Now your future fate is in the hands of these young people. Pierce Budd has forgiven you, though it has been a struggle to do so. But I have one surprise left for you all," said Mr. Bell, stepping to the door. "Regina," he called softly.

In reply, the dark-eyed girl, in a sheer dress of soft, clinging stuff, glided into the room. She slipped straight to the side of the outcast Pierce Budd, and stood there, holding his hand. Peggy looking at her in amazement, saw that the hard, defiant look had vanished from the girl's face, and that its place had been taken by an expression of supreme happiness and peace.

"Tell them about it," said Mr. Bell.

"No. She has not yet recovered from the shock of the discovery," said Pierce Budd softly. "Let me do it. When Mortlake ruined me, and I fled from my former surroundings," he said, "I left behind me a baby girl. Mrs. Mortlake, a good woman if ever there was one, took care of that child. All this I have only just learned. She grew up with the Mortlake's, and when that man's wife died he did the only good thing I've ever heard of him doing — he took care of her and brought her up as his daughter. To-day in the hut you saw me looking at her closely. It was because I thought I recognized a bit of jewelry — a tiny gold locket she wore. It contained the picture of her mother, who died soon after her birth. When I heard her name was Regina, and on the top of that heard you mention the name of Mortlake, I knew that fate, in its strange whirligig, had brought my daughter back to me."

"To-night, with Mr. Bell, I sought her, and she has consented to forgive me for my years of neglect. The rest of my life will be spent in atoning for the past. That is all."

His voice broke, and Regina—a different Regina from the old defiant one, gazed up at him tenderly.

"So," said Mortlake, "I'm left alone at last, eh? Regina, haven't you a word for me? Won't you forgive me for deceiving you about your father all these years?"

"Of course I forgive, freely and wholly," said the girl, stepping toward him, "but it is hard to forget."

Very tenderly, Mortlake raised her hand to his lips and kissed it. Then he drew himself erect.

"What do you want to do with me?" he said defiantly. "I've confessed everything. Why don't you call the police?"

"Because we want you to have a chance to be a better man," said Mr. Bell. "The past is over and done with. The future lies before you. You can make it what you will—bad or good, we shall not interfere with you."

Mortlake looked at them unsteadily. Then his voice broke and he stepped quickly toward Budd. The recluse of Lost Brig Island extended his lean palm and met the other's outstretched hand half way.

"I bear no grudge, Mortlake," he said. "You will always be welcome at our home—Regina's and mine."

"Oh, yes—always," cried the girl, with a catch in her voice.

"Thank you," said Mortlake simply. "I don't—I don't dare trust myself to, speak now; to-morrow, perhaps——"

He strode abruptly through the door and was gone.

Old Mr. Harding arose to his feet.

"After this affecting tableau, is there anything you wish to say to me, hey?" he grated out.

"Nothing, sir," said Mr. Bell, turning his back upon the wizened old financier. "I have seen to it that the money taken from them has been returned to the Galloways."

"Then, I'll bid you good-night, too, since you seem to have taken possession of these rooms. Come, Fanning."

Without a word, Fanning shuffled across the room and reached his parent's side. Not till they were both at the door did he speak. Then, with a malevolent look backward, he paused.

"Roy Prescott," he said, "you've always beaten me out—at school, at college, and twice since we've both lived in Sandy Beach. There'll be a third time, and you can bet that I'll not forget the injury you've done me. Good night."

He was gone, a sinister sneer still curling his lip.

"Well," said Mr. Bell, looking round him with a smile, "who says that all the adventure and excitement is in the West?"

"Not the Girl Aviators, certainly," laughed Peggy, stealing a look at Regina. The girl colored, and then, after a visible effort, she spoke.

"I want to say something," she said, and stopped. Her father bent on her an encouraging look. Bravely she nerved herself, and went on.

"It—it was I who dressed up like you that night, Roy Prescott, and—and I'm awfully sorry."

"Oh, that's all right," said Roy uneasily, and then, "say, you can run like a deer!"

In the laugh which followed they left the room and adjourned to a jolly supper, at which, who should walk in but Aunt Sally Prescott and Mr. and Mrs. Bancroft. They had been reached by telegraph early that morning, and had started on the next train to Roy. How the hours flew! It was almost midnight before they knew it. In the midst of the feast, a waiter brought in a message to Mr. Bell. The mining man excused himself and left the room for a short time. When he returned he was smiling.

"I've just signed on two new workmen for the mine," he said, "and I think they'll make good."

"Who are they?" asked Roy.

"Well, one answers to the name of Eccles. The other was, on one occasion, a foreign spy, but he bears the very American name of Palmer. They leave for the West to-night."

How the Prescott aeroplane, under Roy's management, captured the coveted highest number of marks for proficiency, and how a sensation was caused by the sudden withdrawal of the Mortlake aeroplanes from the naval contest, all my readers are familiar with through the columns of the daily press. The paper, though, didn't print anything about an offer made by Pierce Budd to Eugene Mortlake to finance the Cobweb type of machine. Needless to say, the offer was not accepted. Mortlake, a changed man, is now building and selling aeroplanes in a far eastern principality, and they are good ones, too. No letters are more welcome than those that arrive occasionally from him and are delivered at Pierce Budd's home in New York.

Under Lieutenant Bradbury's kindly auspices, Roy instructed a class of young seamen in the management of the Prescott type of aeroplane, which has become the official aero scout of the United States Navy. From time to time improvements are added.

But, as the young officer says:

"It was really the Girl Aviators' Sky Cruise, that won out for the Prescotts."

And here, though only for a brief period, we must bid au revoir to our young friends. But we shall renew our acquaintance with them, and form some new friends, in the next volume of this series. This book will be replete with adventures encountered in the pursuance of the wonderful new science of aviation, as yet in its infancy. In the clouds and on the solid earth, the Girl Aviators are destined to have some more eventful times. What these are to be must be saved for the telling in—The Girl Aviator's Motor Butterfly.

The End

Milton Keynes UK
Ingram Content Group UK Ltd.
UKHW010625250923
429338UK00004B/328